T0197358

Fiddle for the Dead

Fiddle for the Dead

An Emily Blossom Mystery

BLANCHE RENARD PUTZEL

FIDDLE FOR THE DEAD
AN EMILY BLOSSOM MYSTERY

iUniverse books may be ordered through booksellers or by contacting:

iUniverse
1663 Liberty Drive
Bloomington, IN 47403
www.iuniverse.com
1-800-Authors (1-800-288-4677)

Because of the dynamic nature of the Internet, any web addresses or links contained in this book may have changed since publication and may no longer be valid. The views expressed in this work are solely those of the author and do not necessarily reflect the views of the publisher, and the publisher hereby disclaims any responsibility for them.

Any people depicted in stock imagery provided by Thinkstock are models, and such images are being used for illustrative purposes only. Certain stock imagery © Thinkstock.

ISBN: 978-1-5320-2727-7 (sc)
ISBN: 978-1-5320-2726-0 (e)

Library of Congress Control Number: 2017911294

Print information available on the last page.

iUniverse rev. date: 09/18/2017

To my parents, Max and Nell.

They taught me to appreciate the art of a good story.

Last Chapter First

BLACK SKY

A file lay open on the inspector's desk.

Only one scrap of paper remained.

The letter was not addressed to anyone in particular and was not signed. Indeed, only part of the page remained intact. Half of the script was missing. There was no reason to shred it.

The handwriting was difficult to decipher, but the message was quite clear:

> By the time you receive this letter,
> you will already suspect
> my ending and your beginning.
> Stories are rarely what they seem.
> While falcons
> out of sight,
> the downy dove
> by the silvery light.
> Would that we were
> cast adrift.

Inspector Allard was satisfied that he had avoided exposure of the case to investigative journalists, effectively suppressing the potential of uncontrollable public hysteria. His superiors would be pleased. National security was no longer at risk.

The detective shut the folder stamped "Case Closed."

He stood up, flicked off the light and locked the door behind him.

Chapter 1

CRESCENT MOON WANING

"Only magic or madness would draw folks out of their cozy homes on such a night," mused Emily Blossom.

"Probably a bit of both," said Pete Picken, who accompanied his friend to the event in spite of his better judgment.

Emerald Hill was not big enough to support a real theatre, so the high school gymnasium was the venue for the Greatest Magic Show on Earth. Emily watched the hall fill with hooded and muffled theatregoers. There was stamping of feet and shaking of umbrellas, the air of dampness left at the door.

Outside, rain pummelled the pavement. Rushing rivulets flooded the streets. Lightning flashed, and thunder boomed all around the hill where the village clustered. Inside, the auditorium was warm, dry and full of chatter.

The excitement of gathering small-town folk was contagious. Even Emily and Pete craved social contact and entertainment. The entire town turned out for a respite from the Canadian weather. According to the poster that had appeared around town the previous week, the show promised to provide "Memories to Last a Lifetime."

Emily Blossom was in the audience that evening because she had decided she needed a lifter-upper and magic just might do the trick. The thought of growing old depressed her, although she would never allow herself to admit it.

A person should never use age as an excuse. If one is not terribly careful, one could easily convince oneself to curl up and crawl into the grave before it's time. Never say die; *that makes life much simpler.*

She had cajoled Pete into a date. From experience, Pete had learned that hanging around Emily was more likely to get him into trouble than not. Emily had to bribe him: She offered a free ticket and a beer after the show. Pete had said, "Make it two beers."

Emily said, "This small town is getting me down. Everyone's stuck."

"Stuck?" he said. "In what?"

"People are so busy talking about everyone else that they can't see the forest for the bushes."

"Bushes?"

"We need to do something new—open our minds, shake off the dust."

Pete's eyebrows furled beneath the brim of his farmer's hat. Emily suspected he pulled the brim low over his eyes to give him an air of mysterious intrigue, as if he knew more than anyone else.

"You don't fool me, Pete, with your cocked eyebrows and squinty eyes. I know you like to get out once in a while too. Let's do something exciting."

"Magic is not my way of finding excitement. Wizards scare me," he said, nervously tapping his fingertips together. "They make me nervous."

"Don't be silly," Emily said, regretting her words as soon as they were out of her mouth.

"Then go to your own damn show," he said, reacting more quickly than she'd anticipated.

She had hit a sensitive nerve. She figured she should make it up to him, but sometimes she tired of placating his ego. "Look, Pete—don't come if you don't want to. I'll give my ticket to someone else and stay home. I just thought you might like to get out."

"You mean you want a ride. It'll be dark, and it's too far to walk," he said, putting her motives into terms that made sense to him.

She was quick to take him up on his offer. "Yes. I didn't want to admit it, but I don't like going out alone at night anymore, the way I used to," she said. "I bought an extra ticket so you'd take me in the truck."

"In that case, I'll pick you up at six thirty so you can be early. I know you like to see who else comes out to these things."

Emily had not counted on navigating a thunderstorm that evening. However, the blustery weather appealed to her sense of adventure.

The school building was a practical sprawl of brick and glass, and it was situated in the middle of a parking lot, as if to isolate the students from the village and its historical setting.

A blast of sticky, sweet air freshener in the lobby greeted visitors, effectively masking any smell of human conglomeration. Fake carpets and Plexiglas contributed to an appearance of cleanliness, sterility and control. The scraping and stomping of boots punctuated the din of rattling chairs and cheery greetings. People called out to each other, catching up on the latest gossip. Such an event was primarily a social occasion. Villagers were thirsty to gather news and compare stories of illness, death and divorce.

As background music, Emerald Hill Olde Tyme Fiddlers played reels and jigs in one corner of the stage. They were familiar, traditional fiddle tunes. The piano player started off on a melody with a hammering of rhythm and chords; the fiddles joined in at random. Soon the strings created one raucous flurry of scales and arpeggios somewhat in tune, occasionally in sync and ending on a final discord. The music faded into the bustling hum of the audience, settling in for a good session of gossip and amusement.

Emily chose two seats on the aisle the third row from the front.

"Why do we have to sit so close?" said Pete.

"We want to see how he does the tricks," Emily said with a lilt, as if the answer was self-evident. "Magicians do not want anyone in the audience to be clever enough to see what they're up to. However, I'm sure I'll be able to figure out how he does his card tricks if I sit up front. I'm very devious." She emphasized the last word with a wink.

By now, Pete was used to Emily's quirky vocabulary. "Devious, or dubious?"

"Is there a difference?"

She knit her brows and thought for a moment, pausing while unbuttoning her coat. She could not think and unbutton at the same time.

"Dubious that he'll be able to pull one over on me … and devious like a detective trying to figure out how he does his tricks. I'm both," she said triumphantly.

"How about delirious?"

Emily slapped his arm with her gloves. "Stop egging me on, Pete."

While they teased each other, they scanned the audience to see who was talking to whom, which friends they wanted to catch up with and who was no longer on speaking terms. In a small town, almost everyone knew everyone else, except for the newcomers, who were fresh topics of conversation even before they arrived on the scene.

"I'm sure I know all these people," said Emily. "I just don't know them by name.

"There's a name for not knowing names, you know," said Pete.

"Don't tell me—I don't want to have to remember that too."

A voice sang out from the back of the room, interrupting their banter abruptly. "Oh, there you are."

"Here comes your favourite person," quipped Emily over her shoulder. "I recognize the call of a pigeon in heat."

A woman with saddlebag hips and a bouncing bosom bustled down the aisle, pushing people aside in a rush to close the distance between her and Pete. "I see this chair is vacant. Mind if I join you?"

The ample, clumsy woman stepped on Pete's boots as she stuffed herself past his knees to get to the seat beside him. She wiggled out of her fur coat, gushing in delight at her good fortune. Her plump fingers smoothed her dress over her bulging figure while she pretended to look the other direction. She seemed under the impression that Pete would surely be unable to take his eyes off her voluptuous beauty.

Pete said, "I'm trying to remember who you are."

"Pete, you're just teasing me. Marie. Marie Cartier," she said. "You always forget. We were friends in high school."

"Oh, I'm sorry," said Pete. "I didn't recognize you with all those clothes on."

Marie blushed and giggled, atwitter like a mating sparrow. "You've probably used that line many times before."

As soon as she plunked herself onto the chair beside him, Pete stood up abruptly. "I'm going for a smoke," he said, making a beeline to the lobby.

Marie was breathless from exertion and excitement as she settled into her seat and overflowed her allotted space. Left alone, she had nowhere interesting to focus her attention. She was confronted either by the back of Emily's head or the drawn curtains onstage. Making the best of the awkward situation, she placed her coat on the chair between her and Emily. "I'll just save his place. I'm sure he'll be back before the curtain rises."

Emily continued scanning the room, refusing to succumb to Marie's attempts to distract her. She also concocted a new rule for herself: *Adroit detectives should avoid the aimless prattle of chattering ninnies.* Then she repeated the phrase to herself a couple of times. "A bit wordy, but one gets the point. It'll do," she said aloud.

"What's that?" Marie Cartier's voice had a twang that managed to alert even the most inattentive bystander to hearken in on a conversation that was none of her business.

"Nothing, nothing. I didn't say anything."

By now, all the seats were full, and the audience began to settle. The voices lowered to a murmur. The lights dimmed. An expectant hush descended on the hall.

The fiddlers struck up a strathspey and a clog before finishing with a flare. Then they straggled offstage, uncertain whether to leave their instruments or return to the seats reserved for them in the front row. They whispered and jostled, arguing who should go first and whether to exit stage left or stage right.

Curtains flew open to a collective gasp. The magician stood centre stage with his white gloved hands raised. He was dressed in top hat, a red cummerbund and black shiny boots. His magnificent handlebar moustache and goatee accented bushy eyebrows and sparkling, all-knowing eyes.

"Welcome to the Greatest Magic Show on Earth. Let your imagination take you into a magical realm of wonder and surprise. I will astonish you with tricks and sorcery never seen before. You will learn to believe in the impossible!"

He lifted his hat off his head, reached into the top hat and pulled out a fluffy rabbit with pink eyes and a puffy tail.

Impressed in spite of herself, Emily raised her eyebrows and clapped.

"Have you ever seen this trick before?" Maestro grinned through his pearly teeth. "My little friend has been hiding in this hat for years. Perhaps, it's been a long time since you believed in magic; no doubt, you are suspicious. Life is real, but magic is supernatural. I am a master of illusion. Now is your chance to sit back and allow me to fascinate your senses, to transport you into a world of wonder." He delivered his message in a loud and clear voice with a tinge of a Parisian accent.

Emily felt let down. She had hoped for more originality, less predictability. The performance promised to be exactly as expected. Years of tradition dictated the same tricks, the same illusions, the same feats as magicians had been performing throughout the ages ... nothing more, nothing less.

However, as he continued, she wondered whether he could actually read her mind. He said, "Just when you think you've seen it all before, you are in for a surprise."

She looked around the room to see if others were scowling. The gaping faces of the audience no longer looked familiar. Shadows and spotlights played across the stage, reflecting grotesque and exaggerated features in the audience. The effect was ghoulish and otherworldly. The magician foreshadowed her uneasiness.

"You will be unsettled. Do not worry. You are in good hands." His gloves flashed under the bright lights. "I am not here to threaten your assumptions. I am about to open your minds to possibilities."

As he spoke, subtle changes transformed the stage, which was filling with rolling fog. Strange silhouettes and mysterious shadows lurked behind filmy curtains. An Arabian princess decked with sparkling jewels stood beside the maestro as if she had been there all along. With a diamond in her bellybutton, she swayed her hips seductively as skirts billowed around her bare ankles. The magician's costume transformed without any visible manipulation. The tuxedo was gone. Now he wore a straight-collar shirt with long ballooning sleeves and glittering cufflinks. His cummerbund became a ruby vest with a delicate gleaming watch fob, highlighting his maiden's gold and silver threads flashing in the spotlights. Together they created a hypnotizing aura that sparked like fire in their eyes.

Props appeared onstage where there had been none. Giant toys were wrapped in silver, gold and giant red bows. Boxes, tables, curtains and glass were larger than life and perfect in appearance. The maestro commanded the events onstage with a golden wand. His palms were open, directing and manipulating the attention of the audience towards revelations unfolding in mystifying sequence. Secrets hid in the shadows, enticing, daring the audience to decipher the tricks and flourishes of impossible feats. Exotic music played softly as a backdrop to the hypnotic spell that was cast on the audience.

Emily's instincts as a practicing detective kicked in. She tried to figure out how the illusions appeared so real. In spite of her determination to remain objective, she became dazed and bewildered, lost at the mercy of modern technology and age-old trickery.

"You think you live in a quiet little village where nothing much happens," Maestro whispered. "All is familiar and traditional—a peaceful, out-of-the-way place. Bad things happen elsewhere, on dark continents; crime happens in big cities; foreign nations are at war in ancient lands, on distant shores. Here, you live a normal life. Nothing much happens out of the ordinary. Tulips grow in spring gardens, and window boxes decorate gingerbread porches. You go to church; the ladies serve tea and cucumber sandwiches; gossip is about rocky marriages, babies and funerals. The weather is a favourite topic of conversation. The mayor has breakfast with his pals at the local restaurant."

"How could he know that about Emerald Hill?" Marie whispered.

Emily ignored the comment, hoping that the floozy would not continue to interrupt all the way through the show.

"I am here to convince you that magic exists everywhere, even in this sleepy little village that you tend to take for granted. Welcome, welcome one and all. Now, let me ask you a question: How many of you really believe in magic?"

The audience stirred in the dark.

A small child lifted his hand and bounced in his seat. "I do. I do!"

Self-conscious adults stared straight ahead for fear the magician would single them out. Nervous laughter rippled like a breeze throughout the audience. Neighbours glanced at their neighbours to gauge their reactions. Some blushed and looked away uncomfortably, hoping the great Maestro would not choose them to go onstage as witnesses to the authenticity of the stunts.

"I see that some of you are not sure," said Maestro, pausing for effect. "But you have come to see the Greatest Magic Show on Earth. I will convince you that magic does indeed exist. Magic is real. This is not a hoax. Let your imagination take you on a journey of discovery.

"However, folks, let me warn you that illusion is wondrous. You will laugh, and you will cry, but magic can be very dangerous. The great

Houdini himself died performing his own magic; he was a victim of his own trickery. Sometimes you cannot escape the fetters of life. Magic fools you, convinces you to let down your guard. Be careful of your delusions of grandeur. You must practice discipline. Train your mind to doubt preconceptions."

Emily caught herself falling into a trap. She reassessed her involvement. She reminded herself to practice the skills of a healthy skeptic. *Detectives must be more than clever. One must doubt the obvious and then go even further to embrace the impossible. Think outside the box. That is the key that unlocks mystery.*

"But some of you will be able to see magic everywhere around you," the magician continued. "You will be able to predict the future, control the past, change what you know. You will have the strength of character to achieve the impossible. All you have to do is believe, and your wishes will come true."

The theatrics of the magician onstage enveloped Emily. Maestro's spell enmeshed her in wonderment. The more he spoke, the more she felt like a fly in a spider's web. She felt torn between letting go of reality and feeling the panic of entrapment. Prerecorded suspenseful music accompanied his performance. Smoke and mirrors with mysterious drums intensified the sound effects.

Suddenly a commotion startled the audience. In the dark, someone screamed; another person jumped up. In the front row, a body fell onto the floor. Emily stood to get a better look at the upheaval. She collided with a man rudely elbowing past her; he shoved her into her seat. She felt the sharp heel of his boot dig into the arch of her foot, and pain took her breath away. Before she could recover enough to call out a warning, a sliver of light from the lobby illuminated the blackness of the theatre. A bulky, dark figure escaped through the exit door.

General chaos ensued. The disturbance began in one place, in the shadows, and then rippled like shock waves through the crowd. Eventually, fear and curiosity infected the whole crowd. The magician stared beyond the spotlights, straining to see what was happening in the audience. His arms fell to his side; the spell was broken.

"Lights, lights!" he shouted. "We need some illumination."

"Call the doctor, call a doctor! We have an emergency here."

Emily sat by herself in the dark with Pete's empty seat beside her. Her foot throbbed relentlessly. She was still under the magician's enchantment. Somehow, the collapsing figure in the audience had seemed part of the act. When she heard a woman's scream and felt the vibrations of movement all around her, she was surprisingly unprepared. Usually she was more vigilant of her surroundings. *Detectives should never let down their guard. Even in the most ordinary moments of life, one should never surrender to complacency.*

She quickly came to her senses and reassessed the situation. Her attention gravitated towards the centre of activity taking place one row forward and three seats over from where she sat. She reviewed the sequence of events. A man had slumped forward from his seat. Someone with cowboy boots had tromped on Emily's toes as he pushed past her towards the aisle. He had raced for the exit while everyone else's attention focussed on the body sprawled on the floor. A collective whisper began in the dark, growing into a roar. When the lights illuminated the hall, the crowd's attention focussed on the source of the emergency.

A voice from the back of the hall sounded clear and forceful over the buzz of excitement. "Make way! I'm a doctor. Let me through."

Soon there was a cluster of first responders around the body. The magician disappeared behind the curtain. People began to whisper amongst themselves and craned their necks to see the spectre of a body sprawled on the floor, with assistants huddled around to shield onlookers from interfering with attempts at resuscitation. The crowd parted to allow paramedics access to the patient. Then as their curiosity waned, the noise rose to a roar as everyone repeated their versions of what had happened. Some thought the man had had a stroke, and others insisted it was a heart attack. Some postulated diabetic coma.

Someone took the microphone onstage and announced that there would be an intermission while the emergency response team looked after the patient.

The fiddlers scurried back onstage and struck up some tunes at random. The dance rhythms and marches seemed strangely incongruous with the bustling audience below. The band of ancient musicians performed the same melodies year after year. With little enthusiasm, the players moved bows and fingers by rote. They went through the movements out of habit, as if immersed in long-ago memories that had lost their freshness through repetition. Between songs, they whispered amongst themselves, pointed to members in the crowd, smiled and waved cheerily to their friends. Then the piano player would strike up another tune, and away they would go, fiddling into a jumble of notes scrambling for form and familiarity.

Pete sauntered back to join Emily with his hands in his pockets. An unlit pipe dangled from the corner of his mouth. "They play like they've already died and gone to heaven," he whispered in Emily's ear. "This is a recording."

"The little one in the middle has some life to her. Look at her smiling and nodding, as if she knew everyone in the audience." Emily enjoyed the mere idea of being entertained.

"She has to put on a good show because she can't play. She's air bowing." With a sigh, Pete concluded, "I think I've had enough. This small town do has done me in."

"Well, I won't insist on staying," said Emily, her tone suggesting a mixture of resignation, annoyance and relief. "My foot is killing me. I don't have the patience to stand around and wait for the show to begin again."

She was flooded with a complex jumble of emotions that drained her investigative spirit. She resigned herself to Pete's lack of imagination and was annoyed at her own lack of energy to stay out late on the one night of the year when she actually managed to get him out on a date. At the same time, she was relieved that she did not have to persevere when she would prefer to go to bed early.

They left the milling throng and headed through the rain for home.

Chapter 2

STAR RISING

Even though she had lived on this farm all her life, Daisy Blossom had never been a morning person.

When the sun tickled the backs of her eyelids and the birds chirped as loud as a symphony orchestra, she still resisted the necessity of waking. She snuggled deeper underneath her layers of blankets, where she was warm and secure. However, soon in that semiconsciousness between waking and dreaming, demons of sadness haunted her memories. At this point, she fled towards daylight.

Opening her eyes was a relief. The familiar angles of the ceiling, cracks in the plaster, cobwebs in the corners and rumpled clothes on the floor comforted her troubled mind.

Then she remembered the work of the coming day, and she was tired before she began. She had to stoke the fire in the stove to chase the chill from the kitchen downstairs. A pile of dirty dishes waited in the sink. The animals in the barn were hungry for breakfast. The day's chores had not yet begun.

Canadian winters were brutally cold and long. During the months of deep freeze, things could go horribly wrong very quickly. Pipes could freeze and burst overnight. Little animals caught out in the cold could be dead by morning. Endless armloads of wood were needed for constant refuelling of the stoves to keep the house warm. Nothing was easy. The list was endless.

Now that spring was on the threshold, Daisy would not let down her guard just yet. The weather changed from lamb to lion with little warning. She still wore socks and a hat to bed. She pulled on her long johns before donning her coveralls. She knew that severe changes in temperature were the most stressful for her animals too. Pneumonia and fever were high risk when Canadians, humans and animals alike, emerged from hibernation. Deep fatigue lowered her energy levels. She was not quite ready for the rejuvenating enthusiasm of spring's bursting.

She reluctantly left her warm bed and cozy pyjamas. She put on the same clothes she had been wearing all week. No need to do the laundry for nothing; clean clothes would be dirty again as soon as she went to the barn.

Her first happiness in the morning was the sight of her dog's smiling eyes and the exuberant wag of his tail. My Dog Friday was Daisy's primary reason for living. While Daisy eternally questioned the meaning of existence, Friday welcomed the joys of life with his entire being. His enthusiasm caught her up in its wake and carried her towards the pleasures of the unfolding day.

When she came downstairs and Friday was not at the door to greet her, Daisy's heart skipped a beat. In an instant, all the tragedies that might have befallen her beloved companion flashed into the realm of possibilities: He had been hit by a car, eaten by a wolf or shot by the neighbour for chasing cows. In her wildest imagination, she could not have fathomed the scene that did greet her when she stepped outside to look for him.

Curled up on his dog bed, Friday had become a pillow for a sleeping child. They shared his dog blanket. A ragtag girl with straggling hair tucked herself into the warmth of his giant mastiff body. The dog's golden eyes twinkled at Daisy. To avoid disturbing his precious new friend, he never flinched.

Daisy gasped, and the child awoke. Her sparkling eyes shone with an eerie familiarity that sent chills up Daisy's spine. Friday's tail thumped loudly on the floor. The youngster leaped up and attempted to straighten her clothes, trying to improve her appearance.

"Oh, Aunt Daisy, I'm so glad to see you. Your wonderful dog took care of me until you woke up. Daddy told me that if anything ever happened, I should come here, and you would look after me. He knew I'd be just fine once I got to the farm. He told me to explain everything, and he said that you would understand."

"Who are you?" said Daisy through the screen door. "Where did you come from?"

"It was a terrible night last night. Thunder and lightning. But when he didn't come home, I knew it was time. We have a secret code. I had to come here right away."

"Where did you …? How did you get here?"

Daisy looked outside for a vehicle, for an adult, for some indication how such a child had arrived on her doorstep. Morning sunshine glittered in the puddles in an empty driveway.

"I came on my bicycle. My back sack is not too heavy. My dad always made sure I knew where you lived." The child paused, waited, and then she added politely, "Can I come in?"

Daisy recovered from her surprise, opened the door and stepped aside to let her visitor enter. A blast of frozen air chilled the room in a flash. The dog clattered into the kitchen, proudly escorting his guest into the room.

"Of course, child! What am I thinking? Come in, come in. You can tell me everything over a cup of tea, or hot cocoa. Perhaps you'd prefer hot chocolate."

The child picked up a bulging backpack and pushed past Daisy. She stumbled into the kitchen, gazed around her in wonderment and then thudded her load of belongings against the furniture. She wore blue jeans with bulky rolled cuffs and a plaid shirt. Her silken hair fell around her shoulders in unruly curls, and bangs tickled her eyelashes. She looked as delicate as a porcelain miniature, but her mannerisms displayed unusual self-confidence for a child so young and finding herself in strange surroundings.

"What a beautiful place you have," said the small person gazing around the room curiously. "Everything is so old and quaint."

At first, Daisy took the comment as an insult. She saw mostly a mess: papers strewn on the table with no room for plates; every surface overflowing; antique cupboards filled with dusty knick-knacks; the counter piled high with dirty dishes. Then she realized the statement was a compliment. From a child's point of view, her familiar kitchen took on a new light. The youngster's face glowed with appreciation.

"Daddy said I would just love it here, and he was so right! Thank you for having me."

What a queer phrase, Daisy thought. Her intuition warned her that under the circumstances, she might be the one to be had. At her advanced age, she had learned to see herself as a person of many levels. On the surface, she was calm and gentle. She welcomed strangers into her home and offered the comfort of country hospitality. However, because she had lived alone for most of her life, she was also suspicious by nature. An ill-intentioned treasure hunter might consider her a vulnerable target. She prided herself on her inner strength and remained on guard even in the most innocent of situations.

Daisy navigated around the pile of baggage the child deposited at the entrance and asked, "Who are you?"

"My name is Aster Blossom."

"Who is your father?"

"Jack Blossom."

"You're Jack's child?"

"Yes," said the girl shyly. "We've never met."

Daisy tried to place the child's connection to the Blossom lineage. "Jack's family comes from the other Blossoms, related through my father's father."

"Jack told me to call you Auntie Daisy," said the child matter-of-factly, with a shrug of the shoulders that meant there was nothing further to discuss on that topic. "He always told me, since I was little, that if anything ever happened to him, I should come here. He said you would look after me until he came back. So here I am."

Daisy did not understand what Aster was saying. She saw the lips move and heard the words, but she could make no sense of their meaning. Nothing about the child's appearance on her doorstep made sense to her. Jack had disappeared years ago, and no one had heard a word from him since. Now, this tiny person was standing in her kitchen, calling her Auntie and feeling safe and completely at home here.

Daisy did what she usually did when she was overwhelmed and at a loss as to what to do. Whether faced with grief, anger, gossip or a suffering animal, she reacted in the same manner: Prepare tea. She said, "We'll have time to get acquainted later. Now it's time for tea and a bite to eat."

Daisy fussed around the kitchen. Hospitality was second nature to her; she felt obliged to make a person feel welcome in her home, even though she was uncomfortable with strangers. A sign above the door read, "Nourish the stomach, and you'll feed the soul."

First things first. She performed the ritual of preparing the kitchen for the morning activities, as she had done for 40 years since her parents had turned over the farm operations to her.

She bustled around the kitchen, performing her morning routine. She lit the fire that she had kindled in the wood stove the night before. Soon the room filled with the smell of smoke and cozy warmth. She put the kettle on to boil while selecting her favourite teapot from the shelf. Even though it had a chip on the spout, the size was just right for two tea bags; it was excellent for brewing the appropriate strength for a perfect cup of tea. She moved aside the papers on the table to make room for breakfast dishes, placing a large jar of honey and a pitcher of cream in the centre of the table.

This morning she changed her routine to accommodate her unexpected guest. She set the table for two, located the cookie jar amongst bowls and pitchers on the shelf and arranged a pile of cookies on her grandmother's flowered plate.

"Cookies are not really proper for breakfast, but why not celebrate your visit with dessert? Then we'll have some eggs and toast, and start the day right," Daisy said. She offered Aster a large chocolate chip cookie, and then she settled into the business of preparing their meal.

Aster contentedly consumed the cookie while Friday helped himself to every crumb that dropped into her lap. She chewed slowly and deliberately, pausing when curiosity got the better of her.

All strangers to this kitchen were under surveillance. The dog stretched his body to full length underneath the table, his tail wagging in response to the child's slightest movement. A white cat with twitching whiskers watched her from its throne in the rocking chair next to the wood stove. A dusty-rose dove surveyed her from the top of a cupboard. Inquisitive, the bird tipped its head from side to side, scrutinizing the intruder with one carnelian eye and then the other. Apparently satisfied that this particular visitor was no threat, the bird fluffed up its feathers and cooed softly, as if in tune with Daisy's tone of voice.

Daisy chattered aloud, detailing each step in the preparation of breakfast.

"First we'll get the kettle on. More wood in the stove will get a good boil going. You can't make a proper cup of tea unless the water is at a rolling boil. Then we'll crack the eggs just so. No broken yolks— that'll be good for sunny side up. If I break the yolk, we have to have scrambled. Toast is just about ready. There, you do the buttering."

She handed Aster a butter knife and placed the steaming toast in front of her, demonstrating how to smear each slice completely with a generous slab of soft, golden butter.

In spite of her large size, Daisy moved gracefully around the kitchen as if performing a dance ritual. The wood stove clattered and banged as she manipulated the saucepans to find the perfect heat. Aromas of smoke and sizzling fat filled the room. Soon two plates of eggs and bacon were steaming on the table, accompanied by mugs of tea with milk and honey.

They breakfasted in silence. Daisy was used to dining alone. After lowering her face to the rim of the plate, she shovelled large portions onto her fork and into her mouth. Her cheeks bulged as she munched. Her eyes glazed over as she concentrated on the mechanism of chewing. There was no time for talking. Only after she had wiped her plate clean with a crust of bread did Daisy look up from her meal.

The child ate with perfect manners. She sat up straight, her head carefully poised, her left hand in her lap. Self-consciously she handled her cutlery with precision, even to the point of extending her little finger when she raised her teacup to her lips. She daintily dabbed the corners of her mouth with her napkin. Only her eyes flitted around the room, to see whether the animals were still watching her.

Daisy decided the time was right to clear the air. She needed to know more about the child's background. "Now, my dear, where do you come from?" Daisy considered the question simple enough, but her guest tried to outsmart her.

"My mother's belly."

Daisy tried again. "How old would you be, then? Jack was a child himself when he came to help on the farm."

"Daddy says I'm an old soul in his little girl's body."

Daisy knew she confused easily, but she sensed that the child was playing on her weaknesses. "That doesn't tell me how old you are. I'm trying to place when you were born."

"Some people guess that I'm only 7," the child teased, playing a game that might have been her way of getting attention. "Sometimes I look as old as 11."

"Mmm," said Daisy, catching on. She put her fingers to her lips, squinted slyly and pursed her lips. "Seven or 11? Let me guess that you are somewhere in between. Maybe 9, going on 10?"

"Aw, that's no fair," Aster declared, as if Daisy had spoiled her riddle.

"Who says?" asked Daisy in a tone intended to catch the girl off guard.

"What do you mean?"

"This is my kitchen, isn't it?"

"Yes."

From the slow way Aster capitulated, Daisy knew she could now make an important point. "I get to set the rules in my own kitchen."

"My mother let me make the rules," Aster countered. Daisy recognized defiance. The child was a fighter.

"Really?"

"Yes, and my father says he doesn't care what I do."

"You are an only child, then?

"I was the one they wanted, so they didn't need any more."

"I see," Daisy said, understanding that the raised chin and cocky attitude were a thin cover for the child's insecurity.

Daisy had saved many young, abandoned animals in her day. She knew that right from the beginning, she needed to be firm and gentle at the same time. A frightened creature would lash out when threatened. Tiny creatures needed to surrender, to accept authority without a fight. That was the only way to provide the help they needed to survive.

"Well, around here, if you include all the animals, there are a lot of us to look after. I have rules about safety. We follow the rules. We look after each other. We keep each other safe."

Aster replied, "I was just kidding."

"When I ask a simple question, don't you think I deserve a straight answer?"

"I was just ..."

"Yes, I know, but it's important that you understand." Now she had Aster's attention. "I do care about you. Now that you're here, we have to get along. If I ask you a question, you need to give me an honest answer."

The child stared at her empty plate while a tear gathered on the edge of her eye. Daisy knew she had touched a nerve. The child was more fragile than she had let on.

"Here's the question," Daisy said, pausing long enough for the youngster to rise to the bait. "Will you trust me to find the best solution to our situation?"

"What do you mean?"

"I mean, you are welcome to stay with us—me and Friday and all the animals—until we find your father and get you back where you belong. Is that okay with you?" Aster nodded, and so Daisy continued, "And will you do as I say, because I know what the rules are?" Aster nodded again. "Good, then. Now that we understand each other, we can be friends, right?"

She held out her hand for a shake. The child slowly returned the gesture, and they smiled at each other.

With the conversation finished, Daisy carried her plate to the sink and arranged the dirty dishes into an organized muddle. Aster followed her example and strategically balanced her plate on top of the pile.

"Now, we'll take your things upstairs," said Daisy. "I'll show you to your room. Make yourself at home. Then we'll feed the animals their breakfast."

Her guest followed without question, lugging a pack that weighed more than she did. Together, they installed her luggage in a small bedroom at the top of the stairs.

"I'll just leave you to unpack and tidy up, while I make a phone call."

Then Daisy hurried downstairs to phone Emily.

Detective Emily Blossom would surely be able to solve the mystery surrounding the arrival of her young visitor.

Chapter 3

CAT'S EYE

"Emily, dear, this is Daisy speaking. I know I haven't called in a while. Ever since ... well, you know, since the last time."

Emily replied, "I know this is Daisy. You don't have to identify yourself every time you call. It hasn't been long enough for me to forget the sound of your high-pitched whine. Why are you calling so early? Charlie likes to sleep in. He needs his beauty sleep."

Emily pretended she was an early riser, but her groggy voice gave her away. The annoying phone call had wakened the aspiring detective from a deep sleep. She had been having a lovely dream of adventure featuring her private-investigating self as the brave heroine solving a particularly difficult crime. While holding the receiver to her ear nestled between curlers, she lounged against cozy feather pillows. A pink satin mask that matched her pink pyjamas covered her eyes. Anti-aging cream whitened her skin to the point of stickiness. Her cheeks felt puffy, and her bangs stuck to her forehead.

Charlie, the cat, curled into a fluffy ball on his side of the bed. When the phone rang, he opened one eye just wide enough to assure himself that he would not be disturbed. Soon he was fast asleep again.

Emily was tempted to hang up, but she didn't want to waken her feline companion. He rarely forgave her if he was disturbed before morning. Once awake, the cat was unrelenting. Were she to try to go back to sleep, his methods of revenge were calculated to torture his transgressor. As soon as her eyes closed, he would knead her cheeks with claws extended just enough to be cruelly annoying. To prolong his grudge, he would tickle her nose with his whiskers or, even worse, place the tip of his claw gently but firmly on her chin as she slipped into a deep slumber. Breakfast must be served as soon as he was astir.

After years of being owned by a cat, Emily had long since resigned herself to servitude. *Cats have no conscience. They are the most supreme creatures on earth. Humans are merely their slaves.*

"Emily, I wouldn't be calling so early, but we have a big problem. Things have happened so unexpectedly." Daisy's voice was muffled, as if she were cupping the receiver so close to her ear that her hands covered the mouthpiece. Emily could barely hear her whisper. "The kid's upstairs. I have to talk quickly. Emily, we have to discuss our situation."

"Speak up, Daisy. As usual, you're not making any sense."

Emily's mood was still under the influence of her dream state. She preferred to be the saviour with solutions, not a helpless victim of life's quirky whims. Her imagination tended to rule her approach to situations embroiled in mystery. She saw herself as a detective with a proven track record, above the common problems of human foibles. In spite of her age—or because of it—her contrary nature made her even more determined to surpass expectations. She convinced herself she was a superwoman in the face of adversity.

Emily said, "*We* do not have a problem. *You* have a problem. Let's be perfectly clear from the start. *You* have a problem, and *you* want my help solving *your* problem."

As usual, Daisy did not get it. "No, Emily, this time you're mistaken. *We* have a problem, and *we* need to find a solution. It's a big problem.

Or rather, it's a small person causing *us* a big problem. Emily, you need to come down to the farm as soon as you can. You'll understand when you get here."

"I have other plans today, Daisy. There was an incident at the show last night that requires immediate investigation. And besides, I'll never be able to convince Pete to drive me to your place again, because last time he almost ended up in jail."

"I'll make a lemon pie. Tell him we've got pie and butter tarts, and there's even beer in the beer fridge. He won't be able to resist."

"He won't fall for that again. Besides, what kid? You don't have a kid."

"Emily, that's past tense. You and I, *we* now have a child. That's what this is all about. We need to talk."

"Daisy, dear, need I remind you? Neither you nor I have ever had children, and we are both far beyond adopting at this time of our lives."

"If you can't come to the farm, we'll meet you at the Country Kitchen. The whole village will know about the situation soon enough, anyway."

"Know about what situation?" Emily's curiosity got the better of her. "Daisy, what are you babbling on about?"

"We'll be there around ten. Here she comes—I have to go."

"What are you talking about?"

Dial tone. Emily did not even waste her energy being annoyed. Daisy was a nutcase; that was all there was to it.

After replacing the receiver gently on its cradle, Emily slipped beneath the covers and pulled the blankets over her head slowly, so as not to upset the feline beside her.

A good detective needs her beauty sleep.

Chapter 4

WHISPERED WELCOME

The chore coat that Daisy found for Aster swallowed the small child into its warmth like a smelly hug. Daisy gathered up her own tattered jacket from the arm of the chair by the door and headed towards the barn. Her small companion followed in her footsteps. Friday leaped over puddles, slipping and sliding on the mud, galloping and barking at a crow that flapped lazily over the farmyard.

"He's making way for the royalty," Daisy explained. "He has to clear the barnyard of the riff-raff. Good dog, Friday. You're the best top dog on this farm."

"Do you have any other dogs?" Aster asked.

"Oh, no. But he likes to be told he's the best of the best—makes him feel important."

The heavy barn door groaned when Daisy threw her weight behind the latch. Daylight spilled along the aisle; a cloud of dust sparkled in the sunlight like stars. Aster was engulfed by a waft of odours: hay, manure, animal fur, fermented grain, mould. Daisy seemed not to notice. Their arrival was greeted by rustling, nickering and a general flurry of excitement in the shadows.

As they entered the barn, Aster had the impression she was stepping into an enchanted world inhabited by mythical creatures. Curious eyes watched her approach. They waited, sniffing for clues: friend or danger? Hesitating, they relied on Daisy's demeanour to read the body language of the stranger in their midst. The young girl's instinct was to move slowly, to stand back, to hesitate.

"That's good," Daisy said. "Take your time. You'll see. Everything's going to be all right."

Aster felt reassured and she relaxed. She stopped holding her breath. Her eyes adjusted to the dim light. She began to discern animals in the stalls, as well as a variety of chickens and feathered fowl in the rafters.

Then she realized that Daisy was not actually speaking to her.

They were standing in front of a stall where an unidentified occupant was hiding in the darkest back corner. Daisy had her hand resting gently on the lip of the door, just inside the pen. She waited quietly without moving. Eventually, a furry creature with a long neck and pointed, fuzzy ears emerged from the shadows. Beady eyes with long eyelashes surveyed the motionless fingers. The animal had a long nose, and its teeth protruded from underneath two split upper lips, which seemed to explore strange objects by touching and smelling.

"You don't need to be afraid of Aster." Daisy spoke as if to a friend. "She won't hurt you. You'll see. She's a walking carrot."

The animal made a gurgling sound deep in its throat.

"Now, now," cautioned Daisy. "Don't be like that."

She moved away from the stall and continued down the aisle, speaking to Aster over her shoulder. "That's Llarry the llama. He failed petting zoo. When the people didn't feed him, he spit on them."

Aster glanced back to see the llama's head poking out over the stall door, watching her retreat. She suspected he was disappointed at the failed opportunity to spit on a new, unsuspecting victim. She ran to catch up with Daisy, who had moved down the hall.

"What did you mean by a walking carrot?"

"For most of the animals, carrots are the best treat," said Daisy, as if the fact were common knowledge. "They're very fond of anyone who brings carrots." She stood beside two box stalls, where a horse and a pony nuzzled at Daisy's extended empty palms. "Here we have Bella and Alie. They used to give riding lessons."

"Does anybody ride them?" Aster asked hopefully.

"They're retired; they earned their keep. Now they are a permanent fixture."

Two horses nickered when Daisy picked up two flakes of hay.

Aster adored horses. She read every horse book in the library, and she dreamed of the day when she would have her own pony. She held out her hand and let each horse sniff her in turn. Then she reached up to stroke their necks, one after the other.

Daisy stood by, evaluating the girl's manner with the animals.

"My dad loves horses," the girl said quietly, as if telling secrets.

"Of course he does. He had a way with them when he was a boy," said Daisy. "They're in his blood. Are you the same?"

Aster nodded eagerly.

Alie, the pony with a fuzzy mane and forelock covering her eyes, pinned her ears back and showed her teeth at Bella with a loud squeal.

"Jealous, are we?" said Aster, without realizing that she was speaking to the pony like Daisy did.

Daisy threw the hay into each corner, and the horses settled down to munching on their breakfast.

"Alie's real name is Always Christmas, but she was a difficult little pony. All the kids thought that because she was so cute, she'd be easy to ride. She made it her business to teach little children how to ride the worst pony in the world. She's still cute and still cranky."

"Can you blame her?" said Aster. "I would be too if I had to put up with brats all day long."

Daisy smiled at the child. "You're not a brat sometimes?"

Aster glanced up at her from the corners of her eyes. A smile tickled the edge of her lips. "Maybe sometimes," she admitted.

"Time to feed everyone," said Daisy. "They'll bang down all the doors if we don't hurry up."

She introduced each animal as she distributed grain into feeding troughs in each pen.

"This is Hot Shot. She failed turkey school. This is Percival McGuinty the Third; every peacock on this farm has the same name. This is Biddy Hen. She doesn't lay eggs anymore, but she's too old and tough to put in a pot."

Friday accompanied them as they moved through the chores. Every once in a while, he took off after a cat or wayward chicken, to demonstrate that he was a working farm dog.

Two sheep extended their heads towards Daisy for a pat and a cuddle.

"Rosie the sheep has only one tit; still she raises triplets every year," Daisy explained as she scratched each one behind the ears. "Onion is named for Pete Picken, who says you should always have onions three times a day."

"I thought sheep were skittish," said Aster. "I read that in a book somewhere."

"Shows you what books know," said Daisy. "Rosie and Onion don't know how to read. They just do what they do."

Soon the barn settled into a hush of chewing and crunching as each animal received their breakfast. When the animals had feed and water, Daisy sat down on a bale of hay in the aisle. There was just enough room for Aster to wiggle in beside her. They listened to the rustle of peaceful contentment.

"It's just like magic," Aster said.

Daisy looked down at her with a knowing glance. "Call it what you will."

"It's as if all the animals can talk, as if they are people too."

"Thank goodness they're not like humans," said Daisy with firm conviction.

"I see why my dad loved it here."

Aster snuggled closer to Daisy and gave her a hug. Her arms reached only partway round Daisy's ample middle.

Aster was disappointed when Daisy finally said, "That's it, that's all. Everybody is fed and watered. Emily will be waiting for us at the Country Kitchen. Time to go."

"Who's Emily?" Aster tried to match her step to Daisy's as they strode across the barn yard back to the house. Her legs were not long, and she had to trot along to keep up.

Daisy paused and turned to face the child. She squatted and put her hands on Aster's shoulders, as if to be on the same level as the child. Aster did not like the gesture. She rolled her eyes and looked away from Daisy's piercing stare.

"Emily is my sister-in-law. She's family too. She will help us decide what to do with you."

Aster's eyes watered in spite of her efforts to control her emotions. "My daddy said I could stay here," she said in a small voice.

Daisy stood up, obviously exasperated. Her voice lost its soft lilt and had a sharp edge to the statements. "Your daddy is not here, and he knows nothing of my situation." She sniffed and raised her chin to adopt an air of pained authority. "I'm an old lady. I'm too old to look after a child. You need a lot more than I can provide, and we need to find your parents. Emily will come up with a plan."

Aster studied Daisy's rolling gait as she moved towards the kitchen door. She had not noticed that the woman limped, or that she hunched her shoulders to one side. The dog trotted along beside his master, gaily wagging the white tip of his tail.

Tears rolled down the young girl's cheeks. She did not bother to wipe them away.

Chapter 5

STAR-STRUCK

Daisy leaned all her weight against the truck door and lifted the handle with two hands. The hinges gave way with a groan. Aster smelled odours of burnt motor oil, stale hamburger and barn clothes. The floor was cluttered with remnants of coffee cups, invoices and spare tractor parts. The child had to climb onto the running boards while grabbing for a hoist in order to scramble into her passenger's seat. Her feet dangled above the debris. As Daisy reached across her small body, Aster caught a whiff of sweat mingled with wet wool of an earthy sweater. She longed for the tenderness of a warm hug; instead, the safety strap grazed her neck, choking her.

Daisy chattered above the booming motor, as if she were determined to fill the space between them with meaningless words to avoid any uncomfortable discussion. "My, my, what a beautiful day! We certainly have been lucky with the weather lately. Spring is surely on its way. I'm sure we will have a good haying season as long as it doesn't rain all spring, like it did last year. Good hay in the barn is like money in the bank. There's nothing more satisfying to a farmer than healthy, well-fed animals."

From Aster's viewpoint, scrunched down into the seat with broken springs, all she could see were the tops of the skeletal trees floating by the window, like dancing soldiers with their fingers in the air.

Sometimes a roof and chimney would float across the sky. A hawk glided overhead above the path of the truck before veering off in search of a hapless mouse far below. The clouds were puffy cotton balls against a lazy blue sky.

Blue was Aster's favourite colour; it was the colour of a robin's egg, solid and fragile at the same time. When she was 6, she remembered the feel of a tiny bird's egg in the palm of her hand before she squeezed it with too much enthusiasm; it turned into a dripping puddle of orange and broken shell. Ever since then, she treasured the colour blue.

"When the countryside is covered in snow, we always forget what it will look like when summer comes. The seasons like to play games with our senses. Winter is like a crystal wonderland. Then before we know it, the flowers will be out, and the grass will be as green as velvet. What do you think?"

Aster studied Daisy's sagging cheeks and straggly hair. The old woman looked to the youngster like a bedraggled puppy too muddy to hug.

"I think adults like to talk," she said. "Especially when they're nervous. They talk too loud, as if all of us kids are hard of hearing."

Daisy tucked her hair behind one ear and focussed hard on the road ahead. "I'm not nervous," she said with a pout, as if her feelings were hurt. "I was just trying to make you feel more comfortable. After all, we really don't know each other very well. I thought we could talk about something we both have in common, like the weather."

Aster sniffed. "Just because I'm a kid doesn't mean I'm stupid."

Daisy stole a glance at the small person staring out the window. "Stupid is the last thing I'd think about you." She paused and tried another tack. "How old did you say you were?"

"I didn't say." Aster was unrelenting. "You did."

"I guessed 9 going on 10, didn't I?" continued Daisy, blithely venturing into dangerous territory.

Aster's response was lightning quick. "How would you like it if I guessed you were 99 going on 100?

Aster could feel Daisy looking down at her with penetrating patience.

"I see your point, young lady, but I sense you are not quite as tough as you would like me to believe. Still, it's no excuse to be rude. Snooty does not become you."

Aster sniffed again in defiance.

"I have no experience speaking to rebellious children, but from dealing with stubborn animals, I know I will be no further ahead by arguing with you."

"I thought we were supposed to be friends," said Aster.

"That's right," said Daisy. "But that does not mean you treat your friends with no respect. On the contrary, you should always show those you love more kindness and caring, not less."

"You want to send me away," Aster said with her chin tucked into her shirt.

Abruptly, Daisy pulled the truck over to the side of the road. With her hands still on the steering wheel, she stared at the small person sulking beside her. Aster glanced up at her with tears in her eyes. Daisy reached over and cradled the child's delicate hands in her calloused palms.

"My child," Daisy began. She faltered and then began again. "I'm not sending you anywhere unless you agree. That's what friends are all about. We work together to find the best way for each of us to live our lives to the fullest. I would never hold you back from finding happiness. What kind of a friend would I be if I made you stay tucked away down on the farm, when you could see the world and learn what lies ahead for you beyond this tiny village?"

"Daisy, I don't want to leave you!" wailed Aster, throwing her arms around Daisy's neck. "I want to stay with you, with Friday and the animals!"

"Oh, child," Daisy said as tears rolled down her cheeks. "You have no idea what you're saying."

Aster stayed for a moment in Daisy's arms until the cab of the truck became stifling. The motor droned. Daisy resumed driving. Silence settled between them as the pickup chugged uphill, entering the town limits.

As if it was an afterthought, Daisy spoke softly. "Emily will know what to say to you. She will explain the situation."

The girl looked up at her with wide eyes. She cocked her right cheek to the side and curled her lip. "I have nothing to say to Aunt Emily," Aster said, stressing the word "aunt" a little too loudly and a little too long. "She means nothing to me."

Daisy pulled the truck to the curb opposite the Country Kitchen. She clutched her gnarled fingers in her lap and sighed loudly. "Here we are," she whispered. Then her tone became sticky sweet. "Will you come in for a cup of tea?"

"I'll wait for you here," said the young girl, staring straight at the dashboard with her hair straggling over one eye. "I'm sure you have lots to talk about."

From the corner of her eye, Aster saw Daisy heave open the door just as a car passed on Main Street. The driver honked and swerved, barely missing a collision.

"People are always in too much of a hurry," said Daisy, gathering up her purse. "They just don't watch where they're going."

The clumsy farmer glanced in the side mirror to see if the way was clear. After catching sight of herself, she smoothed back her unruly hair and checked to make sure she had nothing stuck between her teeth. Thus reassured, she scuttled across the street.

Chapter 6

STRAY STRANGERS

Much to Daisy's dismay, when she entered the tiny restaurant, a bell rang, announcing her arrival. The diners automatically turned to see who was on the threshold. Mouths paused mid-sentence; eyes glowed with anticipation. The regulars, who feasted on Maria's homestyle cooking, still craved gossip for dessert.

Daisy felt like a goldfish in a bowl surveyed by a cat angling for dinner. Staring people made her feel conscious of her pear-shaped figure. To hide her bulges, she wore earthy woollen clothes that hung loosely about her large frame. She hugged her purse like a shield in defence, with both arms hiding her farmer's hands. Encumbered by clumsy work boots, her balance was precarious at best.

After searching the room, she spotted Emily at a table in the farthest corner. She suspected Emily chose to sit so far away simply to make it difficult for her to cross the room. Daisy carefully and slowly navigated between the chairs.

"Sorry, sorry," she said, "Excuse me. Sorry to bother you."

Whereas Daisy easily managed to embarrass herself, Emily Blossom rarely missed an opportunity to highlight her clumsiness.

"My dear, I do admire your consistency," Emily said with unusual cheeriness.

Daisy was taken aback. Such a positive greeting from her sister-in-law caught her off guard. She sat down too quickly and spilled the coffee onto Emily's lap.

"Yes, you always do manage to spill someone's coffee whenever you come into the restaurant." Emily mopped her lap with a soggy napkin. "Especially mine," she added. "Well done!"

A faint smile lingered, trembling, at the corner of Daisy's lips. Then it predictably faded into distress.

Ilsa, the ever-attentive waitress at the Country Kitchen, appeared to take Daisy's order. Coffee pot in hand, she replenished Emily's cup and restored Daisy's equilibrium with a welcoming grin.

"I'd like one of Maria's delicious butter tarts and coffee, please," Daisy said in a little girl's voice. She folded her hands in her lap and pretended to sit primly in her place. When she assumed the polite manners of a well-brought-up girl, she hoped she might be able to take the upper hand of a conversation.

When Daisy was in Emily's presence, the conversation threatened to spin out of her control. She could not remember the details of the topic at hand, and usually her responses digressed into incoherency. Before giving her a chance to recover composure, Emily launched right into the matter at hand. She was never one for beating around the bush.

"Now, what's this all about?" asked Detective Emily Blossom in a brusque, business-like manner. "You were babbling on the phone when you called this morning. I hate it when you babble. You are obviously distraught over some figment of your imagination—as usual."

"I only wish I were imagining the predicament we're in," she said before Emily could repeat her insinuations. "I don't have a good feeling about the outcome of this situation."

"Never mind your intuition. Give me the facts. Detectives work on concrete evidence, not wild guesses and airy-fairy touchy-feelies."

"Feelings," Daisy corrected under her breath.

"That's what I said," Emily replied. "You're too sensitive."

"Look who's talking," Daisy said with a sideways glance to an imaginary sympathetic bystander.

"Start at the beginning," Emily prompted, as if the suggestion were obvious to everyone but Daisy.

Daisy fidgeted with her napkin, folding and unfolding it in neat pleats, to gather her jumbled thoughts. "The only thing I can fix on is that she is Jack's daughter."

"Who is *she*?"

"The girl who arrived last night, sometime in the night. She was sleeping with Friday this morning when I came down to the kitchen."

"Who is Jack?"

"Cousin Jack."

"Daisy, you have cousins all over the countryside. The Blossoms are like wild weeds. They procreate, remarry and pop up all over the county. Somehow, everyone is related to everyone else. How do you expect me to keep them all straight?"

"Yes, I know it's confusing. I doubt whether you ever met Jack. He came to work on the farm as a kid, when the folks were still alive. You and Don were married and living in the city by then. Jack hasn't been to the farm in years."

"What makes you think this child is his?"

"Two things. One, she said so, and she doesn't appear to be the lying type. Two, her name is Aster. If she really is a Blossom, then she's named after the Aster flower. As hokey as it sounds, the tradition in our family is to name the girls after flower blossoms."

"Could that just be a coincidence?"

"Would you name your daughter Aster with no good reason?"

"You do have a point there. It's quite old-fashioned."

"My point exactly," said Daisy with uncharacteristic certitude.

"So, where does she come from?"

"I haven't got that far. I have to admit, I'm in a bit of a panic. She's the kind of person who would grow on you pretty quick. I know all about that from the animals. If you don't get a home for the strays right away, you get attached. Then it's even harder to get rid of them."

"Daisy, people are not animals."

"Emily, I don't expect you to understand. Humans and animals are just the same. Helpless youngsters of any kind wheedle their way into your heart. The next thing you know, you're stuck with keeping them forever. I don't have any place on that farm for a wayward child. I don't know anything about raising kids, and it's too late for me to start now. Besides, if it is Jack's child, then he should look after his own affairs. He's my second cousin once removed, hardly next of kin."

"When was the last time you heard from him?" Emily asked.

"Once in a while, I hear news about him through one of the relatives. He left home and went overseas. He never even came to Mother's funeral. We haven't seen hide nor hair of him in a coon's age. He was never one to follow the straight and narrow, even when he was a kid. He was a bit of an odd duck. After I took over the farm, he'd hang around and help out making hay in the summertime. He liked to recite poetry and talk about books and history. He was gentle with the animals—not like most boys his age who are rough and macho. He had a way with the little creatures, and he loved horses. He once tamed a colt that Father said was only good for horsemeat. But then as soon as he turned 16, he left home to go travelling."

"He didn't come home again?"

Daisy said, "Like I said, he was strange. Before he left, he talked about how fortunate we all were to live in Canada, how this was the greatest country in the world and how we needed to stand up for our beliefs, our democracy, our freedom. Sounded like a patriotic American, as if he'd watched too much American TV. The next thing we heard, he'd joined the army and ended up fighting wars on the other side of the world."

"So you never knew anything about his married life, about his children?"

"I heard he comes back to town once in a while. The rumour was he married his childhood sweetheart, but there was never any announcement of marriage."

"Maybe he just shacked up with her."

Daisy admitted, "I really don't know what happened to the lad."

Emily scratched her chin as if to improve her thinking. "Why would he bring his daughter to you, Daisy? Is there something you're not telling me?"

Daisy wiggled in her chair uncomfortably. "He didn't actually bring her to me. She showed up all by herself. There she was, on my doorstep. Well, actually, she was sleeping with the dog when I came down this morning."

"Sleeping with that dog? Now I know you're bonkers. Nobody would dare come into your house with that dog outside. Besides, the whole thing is ridiculous. No kid just shows up on some stranger's doorstep. Somebody had to put her up to it."

"I can't figure it, really," Daisy said, sincerely puzzled. "The child did say something about a secret code."

"Whose code? Who sent her—and to your farm, of all places?"

"Jack used to rave about my cookies, and he'd always say, 'Daisy, you're the best. The rest of the world is all messed up. This farm is paradise. If I ever have kids, I'd want them to come live with you.'" Then Daisy looked at Emily in disbelief. "He'd say those things, but I never believed him. He was just a kid. What did he know?"

"He must have had something on his mind," said Emily.

"I don't know," Daisy said. "I never imagined he'd do this. She's just a mite of a thing. How could he abandon her just like that?"

"Why would he?" said Emily. "That's what I'd like to know."

"Oh, Emily," said Daisy in despair. "What on earth am I going to do with the child? I don't know anything about kids."

"Put her in a box stall. You won't go wrong if you treat her like you treat your animals. Those beasts are better off than most people in this world."

Chapter 7

IN THE ROUGH

Pete Picken parked his truck halfway down Main Street, in front of the Hill News. Although he was headed for the Country Kitchen, he made it a point to never park in front of his destination. Emerald Hill was a small village, and he didn't want everyone to know his whereabouts. There was enough talk about town without giving the folks too much information.

When winter's deep freeze dissipated and spring progressed into the warmth, Pete changed his winter toque for a farmer's cap pulled low over his eyes. Cowboy boots replaced skidoo boots, and a red-checked flannel shirt kept him warm enough against brisk winds. His stained jeans frayed at the bottom, where he'd cut them to fit his short stature. Pete was not one to worry about his rough appearance. When looking for a good bargain in the antique business, it was better not to appear too affluent.

He strode with a long, rolling gait that made him look taller and larger than he was. He had learned that when he walked with purpose, people rarely stepped into his path. When an imposing stranger moved out of his way, Pete's prospects for a successful day immediately improved.

He recognized Daisy Blossom's truck parked at an odd angle in front of the restaurant. He wondered why she was in town so early; usually she was still in the barn at this time of the morning. The sight of a child sitting in the passenger seat piqued his curiosity even more. Her face barely cleared the dashboard, and unruly hair strayed over one eye. With the window rolled down, she gazed with a blank expression at a flock of starlings on the hydro wires above the sidewalk.

"You must be pretty special to rate your own chauffeur," said Pete, standing well back from the truck so as not to frighten her.

The child continued to stare into space as if she did not hear him. Pete tried again.

"Daisy's usual sidekick has more fur than you do. I'm surprised Friday let you sit in his seat."

The corner of the child's lips twitched just enough to encourage him. She rolled her eyes in his direction without turning her head.

"I bet you can growl even louder than that dog. Do you bite strangers too?" Pete continued.

"Maybe," she answered, in spite of her best intentions to ignore him.

"So where you come from?"

"None of your business," she said, attempting to recover her distance.

"That's what I thought. I've been to None of Your Business a lot. People tell me to go there all the time. Funny how that is. I suppose it's just down the road from Pavement Narrows."

She smiled a crooked grin, revealing lopsided teeth and a dimple in one cheek.

"I don't suppose a girl like you would like a cup of cocoa? The restaurant across the street makes a mean gooey-in-the-middle dessert."

"No, thanks," she said quickly. "She's in there."

Pete immediately understood that *she* was not in the child's best books at the moment. He decided not to push the issue; he'd find out the details sooner or later. "They do takeout. You stay here; I'll be back."

After stepping into the traffic while cars shrieked to a stop from both directions, Pete sauntered across Main Street with his hands in his pockets. Pedestrians of Emerald Hill assumed the right of way. Drivers waved them through as if time was not of the essence. The locals proceeded at a small-town pace with nowhere to go and no rush to get there.

The bell rang, announcing Pete's entrance. He smiled and slightly tipped his hat to all and sundry who glanced to identify the latest arrival. He strode straight to the checkout counter, where Ilsa was tallying bills. He leaned across the counter, balancing confidentially on his elbow as if he had a secret to tell. After glancing sideways, he nodded towards Emily's table.

"Put one gooey-in-the-middle lemon square on Emily's bill, and one hot chocolate to go," he said quietly. In response to Ilsa's quizzical glance, he added, "I won a bet last night. She lost, so she pays."

As he waited, Pete surveyed the diners. Viola Hardy and the town fiddlers sat at the round table near the window. Suzanne Duval and her deaf mother tucked themselves underneath a shelf laden with decorative teacups. The chubby reverend, who sang "Happy Birthday" to himself, and his skinny wife slurped soup amid sandwich crumbs on the chequered tablecloth in the sun. Mrs. Seguin, whom Pete referred to as the would-be mayor, and Mousey Dora sat in the middle of the restaurant so they could listen in on the conversations going on around them.

Emily and Daisy had not yet noticed his arrival. Pete surmised that they were engrossed in an intense conversation involving the young passenger he had spotted in Daisy's truck on the street.

When Ilsa returned with his order, he left the restaurant without saying a word to anyone.

With a grand gesture and a bow, he handed the bag and hot chocolate through the window to the child in the truck. "One gooey-in-the-middle lemon square, Mademoiselle, just like you ordered," he said with a fake Parisian accent.

"Don't call me that."

"Well, you're not a Madam, and I don't know the word for Miss is in French."

"I never …" she began.

"No, but I just guessed. You look like a gooey-in-the-middle kind of kid. Have a nice day."

He turned towards the restaurant, stopping traffic once again. This time when the bell announced his arrival, he waved with a flourish. He knew everyone in the place except two strangers sitting in the shadows. Usually, he made a point of introducing himself to newcomers in town, so he approached their table with some curiosity.

"You folks from around here?" he asked with his hand on the back of the woman's chair. "I don't believe I've seen you here before."

Wearing a black tailored jacket and tie, the balding man stood out like a city boy in a country setting. He was obviously uncomfortable when singled out by a local. He glanced at his companion and cocked his head with raised eyebrows. Then he rolled his eyes as a signal for her to be on guard.

The blonde smiled nervously. She had broad lips and long, pointy nails painted the same colour as her bright red lipstick. She tucked her stiletto heels under her chair as if to hide her fashion statement, which was so incongruous in this backwater diner. "Well, yes, we're just here on a bit of business," she said apologetically. "We stopped in for a bite to eat."

Pete launched into his favourite topic. "You've come to the prettiest village this side of paradise."

His interest in promoting the village to strangers had more to do with financial gain than any altruistic motive. His motto was, "The more, the merrier—and the richer everyone will be."

He retrieved three pamphlets from the sales counter: one from the Historical Society, promoting the architecture and history of the town; a tourism brochure touting local recreational activities; and a schedule of events for the Emerald Hill Agricultural Society's 160th Annual Agricultural Fair.

"Everyone comes to the fair," he said.

"No doubt," was the dry reply.

Pete persisted. "It's an experience of a lifetime."

"We won't be staying long."

"Mind if I ask what brings you to town?" Pete continued his inquiry even though the pair seemed particularly anxious to be left alone.

"A private matter," said the man impatiently. "We are not at liberty to discuss our business with strangers."

"Nobody's a stranger in this town, sir," said Pete cheerfully. "I get it. You must be lawyers, then, or undercover cops. That's probably it—CSIS or the CIA."

A shocked glance passed between the pair. Pete figured he had hit the mark.

With a glance under the table, he couldn't resist rubbing salt in the wound. "Well, with shoes shiny and clean like those patent leather dudes, you're sure not a farming sort of fellow, are you?"

They both shuffled their feet under their chairs. Her high heels stuck between the cracks in the wood floor, and she grimaced.

Pete said, "Well, you're welcome anyway. Don't let me interfere into your private affairs." Pete stressed the last words as if they were forbidden fruit. "You all come back and stay a while." He tipped his hat.

Then he made his way directly towards the back corner to join Emily and Daisy.

Chapter 8

COLLECTING CURIOS

"So what's the word about the guy who collapsed last night at the magic show?" Pete said, placing his hat squarely on the table between the cups and sugar bowl. He sat backwards on a chair with his arms draped, so that his hands hung limp over Emily's teacup.

"Must you?" she said, pushing his hands out of her way. "Pete Picken, have you no manners?"

"Manners," he said with a smirk, setting his chair in the proper position, "are for wimps."

"Look who's calling whom a wimp?" said Emily, getting her back up.

"Now, now," said Daisy, at risk of becoming a target in the middle.

"And while we're on the subject of wimps," Emily persisted, "you're the one who left early last night, before the show was over." To Daisy, she said, "This brave fellow here was scared of the magician."

Pete replied, "I never said I was scared. I just didn't like the idea of some guy passing out on the floor in the middle of the show. Not a good sign of things to come, you know."

"What guy collapsed last night? Where?"

Pete continued his excuses without pausing to answer Daisy's question. "Besides, I didn't go out to a magic show to hear the fiddlers scraping away on those blasted violins."

"Shush up," said Emily, "They're all sitting over there. They'll hear you."

"They can't hear me. Every one of them is stone deaf. Somebody should be kind and put them out of their misery," said Pete in an even louder voice. "Who asked them to fill in time fiddling while that poor lad was passed out on the floor? You expect me to stick around listening to their dirge as if they were on the sinking *Titanic*?"

"Maybe they actually *were* playing for the dead," said Emily.

"Dead?" said Daisy. "Who's dead?"

"I haven't heard any news since we left," said Emily. Then, directing her comments to the centre table, she asked Mrs. Seguin, "Have you heard who he was?"

The would-be mayor did not even pretend that she had not been listening in on the conversations going on around her. Seated strategically as she was, in the middle of the restaurant, she blatantly eavesdropped and happily shared whatever titbits she gleaned from her nosey tendencies. "I heard he collapsed from a stroke."

"I heard it was a heart attack," said Mousey Dora, competing with her mayoral friend to see who could get credit for the most recent bits of gossip.

"The paramedics put him on a back stretcher. Seems maybe he had a head injury of some kind."

"Anybody see any blood?"

"Does anyone know who he was?" said Daisy.

"Viola said she thought she recognized him, but she wasn't sure. She didn't want to say anything misleading."

"That will be the day," said the would-be mayor, "when Viola actually keeps her mouth shut."

"I heard that comment," Viola shouted from across the room where she was sitting with her fiddle friends.

"Well, it's true!" Mrs. Seguin was always up for a good fight.

"Viola's mouth is like ten miles of bad road," said Pete to anyone who would listen.

"Now, now, dear. That isn't nice," said Mousey Dora.

"What does nice have anything to do with anything?"

Marie Cartier piped up in her high-pitched squeak. "I thought I knew the man at the magic show from school, but I couldn't recall his name exactly. He changed since he grew up, and ..." With a jiggle and a giggle, she added, "I won't tell you how long it's been since we were kids. Way back then."

"They probably went to separate schools together," said Pete.

"Marie always thinks she knows something she doesn't," said the would-be mayor. "She just wishes she had sole possession of some morsel of gossip that no one else knows."

"Do I sense a bit of professional jealously?" said Pete.

Diners throughout the shop tittered like a flock of English sparrows in the spring.

"Are you defending your sweetheart, Pete?"

Pete smirked with the confidence of a confirmed bachelor.

"I ain't got no sweetheart, 'n' I ain' got no strings."

Giggles rippled around the room.

"I heard the honey man has a girlfriend," said Marie Cartier, throwing her titbit of gossip into the conversation flying around the room, as a child would dare another to match her skills.

Suzanne Duval rose to the occasion. "It's about time."

"You wouldn't have any idea who that someone might be, now, would you?" said Mousey Dora, defying the would-be mayor glaring at her.

Marie Cartier twittered, "I saw them kissing in the parking lot."

"Right there, in public? Where everyone could see?" said Suzanne, incredulous.

From the corner table, in a loud voice, Suzanne's mother cupped her hand around her ear and declared, "At his age, you'd think the man would know about the birds and the bees."

"What was he thinking?" said Viola.

"He wasn't," said Pete.

The tea ladies poked until they could get a rise out of Pete, who usually maintained a cool distance when any bachelor's attachment came up in conversation.

Emily lost her patience. "Do you ladies never get tired of flirting?"

The aspiring detective called the conversation back to business. "Pete, do you still have that glove and scarf you picked up from the stranger who ran out of the building before the paramedics arrived?"

"Yeah, why?"

"I just thought those items might provide a clue as to the identity of the perpetuator."

"You mean perpetrator," corrected Pete.

"That's what I said. If something suspicious did happen last night, surely there was a suspect at the scene of the crime."

"I threw the guy's stuff into a milk can in the back of the truck."

"At least one person did not stay around to see what happened afterwards." Emily's tone implied that her next statement should have been obvious. "Just when everybody else was trying to get a peek at what was going on up front, that person made a run for it."

"Emily, you're being dramatic, looking for trouble where there is none," said Pete. He definitely did not want to know about anything involving suspicious activity. He had had enough run-ins with the cops. Hanging out with Emily usually tended to go badly.

"Do you remember what he looked like?" Emily prodded.

Pete considered the similarity between Detective Emily Blossom and a dog with a bone. She was hard to distract whenever she caught whiff of the slightest hint of wrongdoing.

"The guy had short, dark hair. He was clean-shaved like a soldier; a scar was on his right cheek. He was wearing camouflage pants, an army jacket and—oh, yeah, he had white cowboy boots."

"White cowboy boots?" chimed in the would-be mayor and Dora at the same time.

"Who wears white cowboy boots?"

"Well, I think they were snakeskin, probably from the underbelly of a rattlesnake."

"When he trod on my foot, I knew they were sharp heels," said Emily. "The bruise is still throbbing."

"I saw a pair of snakeskin cowboy boots for sale at the Curiosity Shoppe down the street," said Suzanne.

"Curiosity killed the cat," said Suzanne's mother, still cupping her hand around her ear to better hear the conversation.

"That is the strangest store. It's full of junk." Mrs. Seguin freely voiced her opinion about every business in town. "The owner is quite queer."

"Queer as in odd? Or queer as in gay?" said Daisy, entering the fray.

"You can't honestly tell whether he is a man or a woman," Mousey Dora snipped. "He flounces around as if he had boobs and a sexy wiggle. I wouldn't buy anything from a man who dresses like that."

"Maybe he feels the same way about you," said Suzanne under her breath.

Pete admired Suzanne's spunk. Even though she had spent her whole life looking after her ailing mother, she was surprisingly open-minded, especially concerning strangers in town who might have the potential to rescue her from her doldrums. "It's not junk. The Curiosity Shoppe is an antique store."

"Why would anyone want to pay money for old, used stuff that we all threw out years ago?"

"Whoa, whoa, Tabernac!" said Pete. "You're treading on thin ice. Some of us make a living from buying and selling old stuff."

"Some people throw out valuable antiques," said Daisy.

"They're not antiques until they are marked up in price. Before that, they're just old and outdated."

Suzanne added, "And sometimes people are too dumb to know the value of what they have."

"Antoine has some cute little teacups and some great photos of Marilyn Monroe. His prices are reasonable."

"Antoine, is it?"

"Actually he calls himself—or herself—Toni. He has a lot of Depression ware. I love carnival glass."

"That's putting good money after bad, if you ask me," said Mousey Dora.

"Some people's junk is another cat's ass," said Emily.

"Treasure," Pete corrected her.

"That's what I said. Asset is another man's treasure. Look what a Jackson Pollard is worth! Personally, I wouldn't give you a penny for his work, but people pay millions for one painting full of spatters and droplets."

"Pollard? The Pollards live on the Ridge. I didn't know they had any artists in the family."

"Pollock," said Emily. "He lived in New York."

"What do you think those cowboy boots were worth?" asked the would-be mayor.

"Well, you can't get underbelly snakeskin cowboy boots just anywhere," said Mousey Dora. "Who would want them?"

"I noticed the boots when the guy dropped his glove. I chased after him to give it back," said Pete. "When he saw me following him, he ran even faster the other way. He skidded out the parking lot like a crazy man, doing wheelies on the wet pavement."

"A getaway car," said Emily, barely concealing her excitement. "What did the car look like?"

"Jeep, not a car. A black Jeep with a dented fender and torn window flaps," said Pete. "No wonder it was smashed up, the way he was driving."

"Did you notice anything else about him?" asked Emily. "Anything suspicious?"

"You mean like a gun or a sign that said, 'I'm a murderer. I'm your man'? Come off it, Emily. If the guy is a killer, he's hardly going to advertise it."

"Well, someone pushed me down and stomped on my foot when I tried to stop him."

"He was probably headed for the bathroom in a hurry."

"You never know," said Emily, squinting her left eye in a detective-like manner. "Maybe he was running from the scene of a crime."

"You and your crime scenes," said Pete. "I've seen that plot on other planets. Besides, who would kill a person in the middle of a crowd of people? That would be stupid. We're not exactly in a big city."

"Crime often happens where you least expect it. Detectives should never discount the realm of implausibility."

"Implausibility? Don't you mean impossibility?" said Pete.

"Implausible, impossible. It's the same thing," Emily said. "One is unlikely to be true; the other is likely to be untrue. It comes down to the same thing. Detectives should never assume anything."

"Look, everyone," said Daisy, gathering her coat off the back of the chair. "I've got to be going back to the farm. I haven't finished chores yet, and the day marches on. Emily, please come up with some suggestions about the child. I'm at my wit's end."

"Is that the kid sitting in your truck?" asked Pete. "You'll be lucky if she's still there when you get back. She's an angry little bee right now. I wouldn't want to be in your shoes."

"You spoke to her?" Daisy and Emily said at once. "What did she tell you?"

"Whoa, whoa, Esti," said Pete, putting both hands in the air in defence. "Back off and give me a break. The kid needs time to figure things out. She's not telling anybody anything for a while. You can't blame her."

"Oh, Pete," said Daisy. "Please come down to the farm soon. I just don't know what to say to the child. I feel like anything I do is going to be wrong. I can't keep her, and I can't send her away. She has nowhere to go. What on earth am I going to do?"

"*Respire sur le nez*," said Pete. "Breathe through your nose, Daisy-Mae. Don't panic. The kid's not stupid; she'll come around. You'll figure it out."

"Emily, would you find out who she is?" said Daisy. "Can you use your detective skills to get to the bottom of it all? I know you're really good at solving mysteries. I'd really appreciate your help."

Daisy asked the favour with just the right intonation so that Emily would rise to the challenge.

"Pete and I will get on it right away."

"Emily, speak for yourself," Pete chided.

Emily smiled smugly. Her eyes twinkled with just enough sparkle to melt his bluff.

Chapter 9

HIDE 'N' SEEK

By the time Daisy left the Country Kitchen, she felt reassured. At least she had a plan.

For the time being, she would look after the kid. In the meantime, Emily and Pete would find the father. Everything would work out in the end. Then she would return to her familiar patterns.

Daisy Blossom was a person who relied on routine. All her life, she'd followed the same daily schedule: wake, breakfast, chores, lunch, work, supper, early to bed. She never travelled. In fact, she had never spent one night away from the farm. She had no desire to do so. She was satisfied with her immediate surroundings. Each morning when she stepped outside, her heart filled with a sense of wonder. Nature fascinated her. She considered herself keeper of the lands, guardian of her animals—not an owner, but a caretaker on behalf of some greater power beyond her imagination.

She had long since abandoned curiosity. Consciously, she adopted a limited vision of existence. She preferred to deal with elements within her control. She chose to ignore happenings beyond her comprehension. She was mildly interested in current events and political issues, but on a grand scale, she considered that her life was insignificant in the scheme of the world. She assumed that her ignorance and limited education disqualified her from becoming involved in affairs that were none of her business.

Daisy was happy as she was. She did not believe in regret. She refused to feel lonely or unloved. She created her own bubble of harmony with her animals. Only one person had ever pierced her carefully devised shield of defence. Only one man had ever seeded a grain of doubt in her perfect paradise. She was glad she had experienced love at least once in her life. After he left, she was relieved. Long ago, she'd resolved that the relationship would never have been worth the sacrifice of her privacy and independence.

By the time in her life when the child appeared on her doorstep, wrapped in a blanket with her most cherished hound, Daisy had long since come to terms with spinsterhood. She had no desire to forego her solitude.

Neither did she have confidence in her capacity to empathize. She could not begin to cope with sharing the tribulations of another human being, let alone a young girl. Since her own parents had died, she had never cared for any person's welfare but her own. With a penchant for tragedy and sadness, she had enough to do to look after herself. The mere thought of sheltering and parenting a youngster sent shivers through her core.

All these thoughts and reactions flooded to the fore while she sat with Emily and Pete in the Country Kitchen. She needed reassurance that she could cope. Whenever her carefully constructed nest was threatened, she tended to panic and fall apart. Emily and Pete were her security. She thanked goodness for their friendship. Now she could count on their ingenuity to solve the mystery of the youngster's missing father.

For the time being, she would take the girl home for a short stay. They would become friends. They would share cookies and milk. Then she would send Aster home to her family.

As she walked across the street towards the truck, Daisy was considering what kind of cookies they would bake back at the farm. Cars skidded and honked when she stepped into traffic without looking. The truck door clunked open. She clambered clumsily into the driver's seat. Not until she was seated with her hands on the steering wheel did she notice that the passenger seat was empty. The child had gone missing! All that remained was a half-filled cup of cocoa and the crumpled remains of a lemon square.

Daisy's carefully woven plan unravelled in one fell swoop.

Resisting the urge to panic, she turned the key in the ignition and slowly navigated the truck down Main Street, trying to imagine where a small girl would wander. She desperately hoped that Aster had merely gone for a walk of her own volition. She pushed aside vivid thoughts of suspicious disappearance, missing persons and kidnapping. Frightening details of ugly scenarios flooded into her consciousness when she looked at the empty passenger seat beside her.

Daisy's heart filled with remorse. She was overwhelmed with a deep, grieving sorrow that she did not understand and could not accept. How could she have become so attached, so quickly, to a wisp of a girl who had only entered her life a few short hours ago? Why had she not recognized how much the girl meant to her? Why did she not appreciate her funny, loveable ways; her giggle when she was pleased; and that spark of wisdom so beyond her young years? With uncanny intuition, she knew that her life would never be the same again.

Just when she was about to give up and run to Emily for help once again, Daisy spotted Aster waving to her from the doorstep of the Curiosity Shoppe. As soon as she pulled to the curb, Aster ran to the truck and jumped in beside her, chattering breathlessly with excitement.

"Hi, Aunt Daisy. I'm so sorry to keep you waiting. You won't believe how wonderful that store is! The little man behind the counter is so weird, but he's very funny. He has anything and everything you could ever want, or even imagine. Look what he gave me: my very own

Mickey Mouse teacup. Now I can drink tea with you in my very own cup! He's got old clocks, weird telephones, record players with real records, books, old-fashioned clothes, toys and jewellery. He loves to tell you what's special about all the treasures he's collected. I've never seen any place like it before. It's quite magical!"

Daisy listened to Aster ramble on without comment. She headed the truck for home, gripping the steering wheel for security. The child's babble filled the truck cab and rippled out the window into the fresh spring air.

As they rounded Blossom's Corners, she announced with unusual conviction, "We're going to make chocolate chip cookies when we get home. Cookies and milk—that's our project for this afternoon."

Chapter 10

TONGUE AND GROOVE

The Country Kitchen on the Hill was abuzz like bees to honey. Everyone had pet theories about what had happened at the magic show. They discussed who was in the audience, who said what to whom, what tricks were the most popular, how handsome was the magician and of course how beautiful was his wife. Each one had a theory about the man who had collapsed. Each expert witness had a diagnosis of the cause. Several were sure they knew him personally, but they couldn't place his name. They all talked at once, and few listened.

All the while, Ilsa circulated amongst the tables, serving meals, clearing plates and gathering information to relay to Maria in the kitchen. The aromas of fresh-baked bread and Hungarian goulash mingled with the scents of pastries and chocolate. Coffee brewed, tea steeped and conversation bubbled in every corner.

Emily and Pete huddled over the table, planning their strategy for investigating the problems at hand.

"I think the first step is to visit the Curiosity Shoppe," said Emily. "If the suspect bought his boots there, perhaps we can get a description."

"Emily, need I remind you that there is no suspect at this point? We have no reason to believe that anyone committed a crime."

"Yes, but you have the glove as evidence. We cannot let the trail run dry simply because we're waiting for facts."

"It was raining last night. There is no trail to run dry, and one glove is hardly enough evidence to convict someone of a crime that was not even committed."

They were so intently involved in their discussion that they failed to notice Viola standing by their table, waiting to get their attention. She clutched her purse in both hands to her chest, and her lips twitched. Her eyes switched gaze from one to another as if she were watching a tennis match. She was one of the fiddlers who had been onstage the previous night. They both noticed her at the same time and paused mid-sentence.

"May I?" She pulled up a chair and to join their conversation. "I have to tell someone." She spoke in a whisper, glancing over her shoulder to make sure no one else was listening in. "I couldn't help but overhear that Emily thinks maybe there was some foul play going on last night."

"Why, Viola, what would give you that impression?" Emily said, feigning innocence. "I just hate to miss a good chance at solving a mystery. I am a very accomplished detective, you know, with a proven truck record."

"Not truck. Track. Track record," said Pete. "Admit it: you're just hard up for entertainment in this dull, old town."

Viola was uncharacteristically animated. Whenever she played the fiddle with the Hill Old Timers, her expression rarely changed. Whether she played a jig or a waltz, a reel or a hornpipe, in Pete's opinion she was sombre as a cold fish. However, today's intrigue had cheered her up considerably.

"Last night, just before that man fell on the floor, I could have sworn I sensed someone standing right behind me. After we played onstage, I was sitting in the front row," said Viola. "I could just make out a stranger looming over me in the second row. He was wearing gloves and had a cloth in his hand."

"A scarf? What was he doing?"

"It's hard to say." Viola continued loud enough that all could hear. "I thought maybe he was part of the show, that he was going to make the rabbit reappear or perform some kind of magic trick. Before I realized what was happening, he reached over to cover the man's face with the scarf. I couldn't make any sense of what happening. It was as if he was trying to gag him, or strangle him. There was a struggle, and someone landed on the floor. I was so startled that I nearly dropped my fiddle. Someone actually collapsed, right then and there, just two seats over from where I was sitting.

"I said to Herbert when I got home, 'Herbert, it was like a silent movie, as if they were going through the motions, but there was no sound.' When everyone got so excited about whether the fellow had a heart attack or a stroke, nobody mentioned the stranger, as if he hadn't even been there. So I didn't say anything either."

"We didn't hear anything about this. But then, we were in the third row back near the aisle. At least, I was," said Emily, frowning in Pete's direction. "Pete was still puffing on his pipe in the lobby. He missed the whole show."

"I was reconnoitring," he said, wiping meringue from his moustache.

The murmur of everyone gossiping rose to a crescendo. Everyone spoke at once, producing a chorus of conjectures.

"If there was a violent crime, surely there would be a murder weapon."

"Someone would have noticed blood on the floor."

"Maybe there's some kind of special bullet that can kill at close range without spattering blood or causing a loud bang."

"Viola said there was no sound."

"He had a scarf in his hand."

"That's right."

"People come up will all kinds of gadgets to kill each other."

"A scarf?"

"No doubt Inspector Allard will have some expertise that will enlighten us," said Emily over the din, putting an end to the noisy chatter.

"You, not us," said Pete. "You just mentioned the one person I want nothing to do with. If you're going to get involved with the cops, leave me out of this, here and now. There you go with your snooping and prying again. I've had enough. This time, I'm not going to fall for it."

"Pete, I promise I won't get you in trouble with the police again," said Emily in that sticky-sweet voice that made Pete shiver. "You can trust me. I've learned my lessons. Besides, Inspector Allard knows I wouldn't hang around with any shady characters. I'm just an innocent, little, old lady. You know that."

"Little? Yes. Old? Like antiques, the definition depends on how much you can get when you go to sell. Lady? Hardly. Innocent? Not in a million years."

"Well, some people get fooled by my posterior."

"Don't you mean exterior? As in, what you see is what you get?"

"Yes, that's it, but I'm not what most people think I am."

"That's an understatement."

"Thanks for telling us about this," said Emily, patting Viola on the shoulder. "You did the right thing."

Viola's relief was palpable; she had unburdened herself of a great worry. Emily looked at Pete smugly. Pete glared at the ceiling as if there were a giant spider waiting to drop down on Emily's neck at any second.

Emily resumed the conversation where they had left off before Viola's intrusion. "Then we have to call the hospital."

"Oh, yeah," said Pete. "They're about to tell you who the man was and what he was admitted for!"

"No, Pete, of course not," Emily said.

"I hate the way you say my name like that," Pete said with eyes half-closed.

Emily ignored his comment and continued unabated.

"They wouldn't tell us anything about that. We have to phone to see if they have a patient registered by the name of Jack Blossom. We still don't know what happened to the child's father. She never told Daisy what happened to him. Maybe he's in some kind of trouble."

"I hate hospitals. They're full of sick people."

"I didn't say we have to go there. We just have to call and ask whether they have any record of a person listed by that name."

Pete grew weary of the banter. He scraped his chair back and rose to leave Emily to her own devices. "The bill's on you."

"But, Pete, I forgot to bring my purse," she said with a wink and a whine.

"You did? Like hell. Wash dishes if you have to. You're always making promises you have no intention of keeping."

"I always keep my word," Emily cajoled.

"Good—then *you* pay."

Pete sensed that Emily would manipulate his gallantry and her exit so that the others would not think he was tired of her company. Sure enough, she lifted her jacket off the back of the chair and handed it to Pete so he would help her put it on. At first, he pretended not to understand her implication. With a quizzical expression, he exaggerated a hesitation, holding the coat at an odd angle. With an audible *tut-tut*, she placed each side of the garment in his hands as if on a hanger. Then she propped the coat up to her height so she could slip her arms into the sleeves. With a sigh of resignation, he tossed the jacket over her shoulders.

Emily scanned the room to assure herself the tea ladies were watching his gesture of chivalry. She picked up her purse and paid the bill without commenting on the additional drink and dessert Pete had purchased for the child in Daisy's truck.

Chapter 11

Costume Work

In addition to the Country Kitchen on the Hill, the town consisted of a post office, two banks, a pharmacy, a tavern and a handful of small shops. The Curiosity Shoppe was the most recent business to open on Main Street.

Signs on the door announced "Antiques are always in fashion" and "Antoine Garibaldi at your service: your own personal shopper."

Every day a new assortment of curios and nostalgia appeared in the window. On the sidewalk in nice weather, a shelf of women's shoes displayed spike heels and pointed boots beside a bookcase of paperback books. A handwritten sign read "All on Sale for a Looney."

Emily loved exploring antique stores. She enjoyed the sense of discovery while hunting for rare treasures at bargain prices. Inside the shop, hanging chandeliers with colourful shades produced dim lighting that created an atmosphere of mystery and surprise. Victorian bronze statues and art deco figures lurked in dark corners like mute witnesses to adventure. Clients had to navigate through narrow rows of furniture: chests, dressers, bureaus, desks and Canadiana armoires. Shelves of knick-knacks lined the walls from floor to ceiling. In a glass case by the cash register, diamond rings and rhinestones, gold wedding bands and costume jewellery vied for space with Mickey Mouse mugs, miniature tea sets and blown glass animals. A larger-than-life photo of Marilyn Monroe surveyed the store from behind the counter. Every spare wall space displayed a variety of oil paintings, landscapes in filigree frames and modern abstracts alongside naive art decorative plates. Clocks of all shapes and sizes tick-tocked and chimed on the quarter hour. A vague smell of must gave one the impression that here, long forgotten memories clustered in dusty corners.

When Emily first entered, the shop seemed unattended. She wandered at leisure, inspecting each oddity that caught her eye. She was rifling through a wardrobe of evening gowns when she heard a lilting voice sing out from behind the royal purple velvet curtain of a changing room

"I'll be with you in just a moment. I'm just trying on one of my most recent purchases."

Presently, a tall man with shoulder-length platinum hair emerged. He wore a kid leather smoking jacket with green satin collar. One hand cocked on his hip; with the other, he smoothed the clothes along his svelte figure. He had long fingers bejewelled with several rings, including on his thumb, as if he could not decide between one or the other and so wore all at once.

"How do I look?" He exaggerated an alluring wink and tossed his hair over one eye with a practiced sideways tip of the head.

"Very catching," said Emily.

"Eh?" he said, peering through his bangs.

Emily corrected herself quickly. "Fetching. Catching. You know. Yes, you look just fine in that jacket."

A crooked smile curled his lips from one side of his mouth. Wrinkles and sagging, hollow cheeks made him look older than he first appeared.

"Of course I look fine," he said with a drawl. "One just *has to* appreciate the superb cut of this exquisite garment."

His nasal twang accented the *has to* with just the right amount of stress to ornament the syllables. His affectation assumed an acquired right of expertise on the subject of fashion. He took off the jacket with a flare and hung it on a wooden hanger with several other vintage costumes.

"I believe this is your first visit to the Curiosity Shoppe," he said. "May I introduce myself? Antoine Garibaldi, at your service." With a smile revealing overlapped and stained teeth, he bowed with a flourish. "You can call me Toni. And you are?"

"Mrs. Emily Blossom. I'm pleased to meet you. I must say, I'm so very glad you've chosen to open your shop in Emerald Hill. We need a little boutique like this one in town. A bit of class never hurts a sleepy little village, you know. I hope you will do well here."

He raised one eyebrow, betraying the slightest of doubts. "I hope so too. You have no idea how important it is to me that this idea succeeds." Then he brightened, as if turning a charm switch. "Now, may I offer you a cup of coffee?"

"That would be lovely," said Emily. She was surprised to hear herself using a twinge of a British accent. Antoine's mannerisms encouraged pretension, and she rose to the game. *Detectives may find it useful to conform to certain behaviour in order to set one's informant at ease. Make whatever compromises are necessary to obtain full cooperation, while avoiding the slightest suspicion.*

The shopkeeper cleared a place on a small round table by the window next to the entrance. He disappeared to the back of the store while Emily settled herself down to wait. Presently he reappeared with two china mugs full of steaming coffee. "I'm sorry, I'm out of milk. I hope you don't mind drinking your coffee black."

Emily insisted she always preferred strong black coffee before lunch—a lie that seemed to put Toni more at ease.

"I had this vision that all my customers would come in for coffee, and that we would have long chats while we discussed their purchases. It hasn't exactly turned out like that," he said. "I've been open two weeks, and I don't have enough money to buy cream to go with the coffee. I hope business turns around before the end of the month, when my rent is due."

"Where did you come from, then?" Emily asked.

"It's a long story." His sad eyes bore heaviness from many troubles weighing him down. "I'm from across the river in Quebec. I thought that by coming to Ontario, I'd get a break. I've worked so hard to sort through my collection for the best items at the most attractive prices. It took me two months just to bring the stuff here, move in and set up the displays. I sank all my money in this place. It's my last chance. If it doesn't work out, I'm afraid to think what will happen to me."

"Why did you choose to come to Emerald Hill, of all places?"

"I needed a fresh start. I drove around the countryside, looking for just the right spot. It's a pretty little town, situated perfectly: halfway between Ottawa and Montreal, and not far from the US border. I figured I couldn't go wrong.

"I thought folks in the country would be happy to hire a personal shopper. I can go to the big cities to find just what they were looking for. I'm very good at discovering that one perfect item for a special occasion: an evening gown for a party, shoes to match a dress for a wedding, a unique costume for a Halloween party. Believe me, I have lots of experience shopping for quirky clothes. I figured people would be happy to pay me to find them that perfect gift for that someone special."

"You must be very good at what you do," said Emily. "I heard you even sold a pair of snakeskin cowboy boots. How unusual is that?"

"Yesterday was a surprisingly good day, considering the weather," said Antoine with a wistful grin. "The guy hardly seemed the type, but he bought them anyway."

"Who would buy a pair of boots like that?" asked Emily. "Were they really all that unique?"

"It was pouring rain. He said his sneakers were soaked, and he had a long way to go. He needed something dry on his feet. He bought the boots and a scarf. He didn't look like a cashmere scarf kind of a guy, but he bought the only one I had. He looked at that camouflage jacket, but said he didn't have enough money to buy it."

"Was there anything unusual about the man?"

Antoine stood up and opened the door. "You don't mind if I smoke, do you?" He extracted a hand-rolled cigarette from a silver case. "I've been trying to quit, but that's not going to happen. At least, not in the near future."

He handled the silver lighter with long graceful fingers. His rings sparkled in the sunlight. After taking a deep inhalation, he watched the smoke curl out the door towards the street. Then he glanced sideways at the little woman seated at his coffee table, as if assessing her capacity to understand from where he was coming.

"I don't imagine you know a lot about the world I come from," he said. "I'm not sure how much to explain."

"Give it a try," Emily said in as smooth a tone as possible. "I look old, but I'm not a babe in the woods."

Toni paused again before he began his explanation. "Let's put it like this: In my world, I can tell the difference between men who like women, and men who like men in women's clothes. That's how I used to make my living. I was very good at it, let me tell you. Without going into a lot of detail, the guy who came into my store looking for those boots was a loaded gun with no safety on the trigger. Anger was eating him up from the inside."

"How could you tell?"

"People like me have a sixth sense. He got what he thought he wanted. He paid for the boots. But no way in hell was he ever going to be satisfied."

"Will you ever see him again?"

"Does the devil return to the scene of the crime? I doubt it. That dude was on a mission, just biding his time. He left here with hatred burning up inside of him. Nothing was gonna get in his way. I feel sorry for whoever he was aiming for. He wasn't about to miss his target."

"Antoine, can you tell me what he looked like?"

"What's it to you? If you'll excuse me for saying so, you don't exactly seem the type to get involved with a guy like that."

Emily laughed with delight. She loved to be underestimated. She always imagined herself as a cunning sleuth disguised as an innocent, frail widow on the verge of her demise. She felt quite smug when she could deceive a perceptive and experienced person like Antoine.

"You strike me as a man with a lot of street smarts, but you're not all that clever when it comes to, shall we say, women of a certain age." Then her tone of amusement turned deadly serious. She enunciated her words with sharp accuracy. "It's very important that you tell me exactly what this man looks like. He may have committed murder in cold blood. We have to find him."

"Black hair greying at the roots. Black eyes. Six foot. Around a hundred and seventy pounds."

"Any defining characteristics? Tattoos, piercings, scars?"

"A scar on the right cheek. Military type. Straight posture and muscular, as tough on the inside as the outside."

"Anything else?"

Toni paused and grinned, showing crooked teeth. "He tried on a flannel shirt in the aisle. I couldn't help but notice. He had a tattoo on his shoulder that read 'Platoon VX.' There were scars on his back. I suspect he knows a lot about violence."

Emily rose to leave. In her hand, she had a tiny teapot and lid with a dragonfly on a lily pad. "How much is this darling pot? It's so unique."

Antoine hesitated as if debating whether to charge full price or to give it to her as a gift. "Twenty dollars?"

Emily handed him thirty. "Enough for gas and cream for the coffee."

"Nice to meet you, Mrs. Blossom," Antoine said. "Please do come in again."

She nodded politely and shook his hand. "It will be a pleasure, to be sure." She rifled in her purse. "Here's my card. If you think of something I should know, please do leave a message."

Toni squinted at the fine print. "Detective? You don't look like a cop."

Emily willed herself to blush. "Looks can be deceiving, Mr. Garibaldi. Don't you agree?" She winked and paused just long enough so that he could open the door to usher her out of his shop.

Chapter 12

SPECIAL DELIVERY

Emerald Hill's post office stood like a sentinel on Main Street. The chunky, squat edifice bore its Canadian flag properly as an honour guard standing erect among the Victorian brick houses that clustered like pretentious dowagers around the town square. Perched on top of a hill, the town overlooked 360 degrees of horizon, stretching north and east to the Quebec border, and south towards the United States. Mail from around the world arrived in Emerald Hill, a hub for distribution to sub stations sprinkled throughout the Eastern Ontario area.

After her visit with Antoine at the Curiosity Shoppe, Emily headed for the post office to continue her investigation.

Only one person was responsible for the postal delivery system serving all the homes in town and the outlying rural districts. Ida Mailer knew everyone who lived within a 50-kilometer radius. She also knew most of their business, family affairs and travel schedules.

Ida greeted everyone, every day, with the same bright smile and twinkling eyes. She was always cheerful no matter what. She exhibited great pride in her job. She made sure that all the letters found their way into the right boxes, that bills and taxes were predated and that everyone in town knew she thoroughly scrutinized every postcard before delivery.

Some wily residents even took precautions to send postcards addressed directly to Ida, alerting her to their travel itineraries and whereabouts. In short, Ida knew everything about everybody.

The villagers knew that officially, any information Ida possessed was strictly confidential. After all, Canada Post relied on their reputation as worthy of the public's trust. Right to privacy was a cardinal rule if one worked for the postal service. The trick was to pretend not to ask. One had to be very discreet. Discussion about the weather was always a good way to start.

"Are you the one to take credit for this lovely day, after such an awful storm last night?" asked Emily.

"Wasn't that a terrible rain we had? I thought for sure the wind would blow right in underneath the eaves and start leaking down the wall again. We have a paint bubble just under the chimney, where we repaired the walls last year. Last night was a sure test to see if the workmen patched the right spot."

"Did you hear about the magic show, then?" said Emily. "Has anyone mentioned who collapsed?"

"No, no. It seems a bit of a mystery. Mary Rainey was in earlier. She was sitting next to him, but he never said his name."

"Rainey? Is that the chatty redhead who moved to town last year? She collects people the way some people collect postage stamps. Pete calls her the Queen Bee."

"Mary said the man seemed to be alone. He was a bit nervous and distracted, but once the lights dimmed, he relaxed a bit. He actually liked the fiddle music and said he used to play as a kid. A few minutes later, there was a scuffle next to Mary. She couldn't see anything in the dark. The next thing she knew, the fellow sprawled out on the floor in front of her. When the paramedics came in, they could not find any wallet or ID. They asked Mary to give them room to tend to the patient.

A doctor arriving on the scene pushed her out of the way. They gave first aid and then took him away on a stretcher."

Emily tried not to seem too interested in more details. "Have you got some mail for me today?"

Ida left the counter to check the rows of boxes while Emily tried to scan the address labels for the various rural routes, to no avail.

"No mail today, Mrs. Blossom. Only the *Hill News*."

Once, Ida had delivered a letter to Emily's house addressed to Charlie the Cat c/o Mrs. Blossom. It contained a package of catnip from the vet reminding her that Charlie was due for his booster shots.

"That's good. No bills." Emily was relieved there were no other customers at the counter when she slipped in the next question. "Does Jack Blossom have an address where I could mail him a postcard?" She spoke in a whisper, as if she knew that although Ida was sworn to secrecy, she could divulge a little information if it were for a good cause.

"For the little girl, Aster? She'd love that, I'm sure. I think it was her birthday recently."

"Yes, yes," said Emily. "That's right. I just wanted to send a little something."

"They live at the end of the Second Concession, down by the Bog—number 269, Rural Route 2. If you mail it during the week, they'll get it the next day."

"Thanks so much, Ida. You're a treasure."

As soon as Emily emerged from the post office, she paused on the steps to write down the address so as not to forget. To her dismay, the would-be mayor was beetling her way across the street towards her, in full throttle.

"There you are, Detective. I was afraid I'd miss you." Mrs. Seguin was breathless. She waddled when she was in a hurry, with her shoulders rocking from side to side, as if to lend impetus to her urgency. "I just wanted to tell you. No one by the name of Jack Blossom has been admitted to the hospital. I couldn't help but overhear your conversation with Pete about your investigation. I heard you mention that you wanted to know whether Blossom was a patient there. I phoned the registration desk. I thought I would help out, because I know that neither of you has a cell phone. I'm actually surprised you don't carry one. As an important detective, surely you would find it very handy."

Emily did not try to contain her annoyance. She closed her eyelids halfway and lifted her chin just enough to assume authority. "I have no need for contraptions. My investigative skills are quite sufficient without the aid of modernity."

"Well, at least Pete should have one. I'm sure he would do more business selling his antiques. It would save a lot on gas."

"Mr. Picken does not need any interference with his driving skills, thank you very much. He's enough of a hazard on the road without one of those gadgets ringing in his ear." Emily hesitated, thinking better of what she had just said. "But don't tell him I said that."

Mrs. Seguin snickered with glee. "Of course, Emily! I would *never* repeat anything you told me in confidence."

"No, of course not."

Regretting her words as soon as they left her lips, Emily turned her back on the town's most incurable gossip.

Chapter 13

BRIGHT STAR

"I think I'm getting used to having you around, my dear," said Daisy that first evening. "Now that we are getting to know one another, all the animals seem to accept you too. Jewel doesn't take to strangers easily. Yet there she is, sitting on your shoulder, preening her feathers and cooing in your ear."

Aster gently scratched the turtledove around her ringed collar.

"She's flirting with you," Daisy said. She often translated animal behaviour into words for an uninitiated visitor.

"I wonder if Friday could sleep with me tonight?" Aster said. "He was so warm and cuddly."

"No, Friday doesn't come in at night. He guards the farm and wakes up barking in the middle of the night. However, the white kitty, Pippin, loves to sneak under the blankets. She would be happy if you let her sleep with you."

"Oh goodie. Can we go up now?"

Daisy was startled and pleasantly surprised. "I thought I was an old fuddy-duddy, going to bed so early," she said. "I'm glad you're like me. It has been a long day."

She heaved her body out of the rocking chair and unfolded her stiff muscles before she could move to put out the light. To make sure all was safe before leaving the room in the dark, she stoked the fire and shut down the dampers. Aster skipped ahead, carrying the little cat on her shoulder as they proceeded upstairs.

Tucked under the slanted roof was a child-sized bed, covered with a patchwork quilt of autumn colours. A bedside table was just big enough for a reading lamp and a book. While Daisy looked on, Aster unpacked her rucksack and neatly folded her few belongings into the drawers of a tiny antique dresser in the corner. Then the child snuggled down between the flannel sheets, and Daisy tucked the woollen quilt around her neck. The white kitten took no time at all to curl herself in a ball on the pillow.

Daisy was about to put out the light when Aster lifted both her arms from under the covers. "Can I have a kiss goodnight, Auntie?"

Daisy awkwardly leaned down to gather her tiny visitor into a bear hug. "Good night, child. Sleep tight." She heard herself whisper the words from somewhere deep inside her memories, as if such tender secrets belonged only to the night.

Daisy's own bedroom felt strangely unfamiliar this evening, now that a youngster slumbered across the hall. She had a hard time falling asleep, and her dreams were haunting. Unable to get comfortable, she restlessly tossed the covers aside and then piled them high around her. Nothing soothed her anxious nerves.

Around midnight, she had just fallen into a deep sleep when she woke to muffled sobbing. At first, she could not place where the sound was coming from; she had forgotten about the child. She had slept every night in this house ever since she was born. If there were such a thing as ghosts in the farmhouse, she had long since come to terms with them. Because she lived alone, she was used to the sounds of solitude. The cry of loneliness was a stranger to her.

She stared into the darkness until she could comprehend and place the sound into context. Then she slipped out from under her warm covers and tiptoed across the hall. After putting her ear to the door, she listened for a moment until the scratching of the little cat at the door reminded her to knock.

"Aster? Aster, honey? Can I come in?"

The crying continued—louder now, uncontrollably. Daisy gently turned the doorknob and barefooted across the rug. When she sat down, she had to make room for her large bottom without crushing the small body on the tiny bed. She placed her hand on Aster's shoulder and comforted her with the softness she would use to calm a startled animal.

"There, there. No need to cry, my dear. Shh. Everything will be all right. Daisy's here. No need to be frightened. Hush, hush."

Soon the sobbing quieted. The child began to snuffle, catch her breath and calm her weeping. Her pillow was soaked with tears. Daisy stroked the little girl's forehead and brushed the damp hair from her eyelids.

"What is it now? You can tell Daisy. Tell me what's the matter. You will feel better if you share your worries. I'll help you sort it all out."

After several attempts at an explanation, finally Aster put together one coherent sentence. "I miss Daddy," she wailed, bursting into a fresh torrent of tears. "I'm afraid this time he won't be coming back. I saw the look in his eyes when he said goodbye. He told me it was time. I should come to you. I don't think I'll ever see him again."

"Aster, listen to me," said Daisy more sternly than before. "Emily and Pete will find your father. Emily is a very fine detective. They will find out where he is. In the meantime, it's your job to be safe and happy. That's what your father would want you to do."

"Daisy, would you read my daddy's letters to me so I can go to sleep? Sometimes I read them to chase away the nightmares. I have them all. Would you read to me, please? Then I promise I'll go back to sleep."

She pushed back the covers and padded across the room to retrieve her back sack. She rummaged around in the bottom and pulled out a tattered brown envelope. The stamp on the envelope was from Afghanistan, with a return address from Corporal Jack Blossom.

Aster snuggled down under the quilt and waited for Daisy to begin.

To My Dearest Baby Daughter, My Little Star,

I am sitting under a starlit sky in the night. The desert surrounds me; it is dry and immense. All is so quiet that I am afraid of the dark. Tonight is heavy with shadows. The sun has travelled below the horizon, making its way towards morning, where you are waking to your very first day. I am jealous that the sun will see you before I will.

I wish I were there to see you come into the world, to hear you take your first breath, to hold you in my arms, to feel your tiny heart beating so very fast, pacing its steady rhythm to keep you alive for the rest of your life. I wish I could feel your tiny, perfect fingers holding tight to mine. I want to hug you close and whisper in your delicate, miniature ear all the secrets of the earth. I would cradle you in the palms of my hands and gently kiss your soft, warm cheeks.

I would like to get to know you as you grow up and discover the world, but you do not even know yourself. You are just beginning the most wonderful journey that exists … a journey of life.

Some things will be difficult, but the joys and happiness in store for you will far outweigh the worst. If I had one wish, I wish that you would know me ... the best of me. I wish that we could become best friends. We would laugh together. I can already hear you giggling. I can imagine your smile, innocent of danger; the sparkle in your eyes; and your delight in discovering happiness.

I wish I could protect you forever from the evils that lurk in places where you least expect them. I wish I could wipe away your tears, taste your food, change your diapers, see your first step, listen to your first song, dance the first dance and hold you in my arms as you find your balance in the world.

I will be there for you forever, Little Star, as you are there shining in my future. We will travel together, no matter how far apart we may be. I am always your father. You are my branches and my seed.

Know, my darling daughter, that I will love you forever and ever.

Your adoring father,

Jack

"Daisy," Aster said in a tiny, sleepy voice. "Can a person change her name? Just like that, can you change what people call you?"

Daisy hesitated, trying to foreshadow the consequences of whatever answer she might offer. "I don't think there's any harm in asking people to call you by another name. Lots of people prefer to use nicknames."

"Daisy, would you call me Star from now on? I think I'd like that. Aster is so formal, and Star makes me feel more ... well ... more me."

"Of course, Aster, dear." Then Daisy quickly corrected herself. "Excuse me—I meant to say, of course, my little Star. It might take me a while to get used to calling you by the new name, but we'll work on it."

Aster snuggled deeper into her pillow and cushioned her cheeks in her hand. She stroked the white kitten curled into the crook of her neck. With her eyes closed, she said, "Thank you, Daisy. Now, if you read me one more story, I'll go right to sleep. Could you read the one about your farm?"

"My farm? There's a letter about my farm?"

"Oh, yes," Star whispered sleepily. "You'll like this one. It's all about you."

Daisy rifled through the pile of letters until she came to the one entitled Blossoms Corners. She read in a soft and lilting voice.

My Dear Little Star,

There is one place on this vast planet where peace really does exist. Forests abound, flowers bloom and creatures of all sorts live together in harmony.

An ageless old woman is the keeper of Blossoms Corners Farm. Daisy Blossom tends the farm with a giant watchdog as her protector and companion. Daisy surrounds herself with birds of all sorts: doves, chickens, ducks, turkeys and peacocks. She keeps an assortment of tame beasts and loving animals. She even has goldfish in a pond who swim to the surface when she calls them for supper.

Nature takes her course here. Injured bodies recover. Wounded hearts heal. Death is a part of living. Life thrives in all stages from birth to one last final breath.

I know about this place because I was there as a young boy. Work was play in the sunshine of hay fields. Cleaning was fun in the shelter of the ancient barn.

If anything happens to me, my love, before you grow into womanhood, seek out this place of beauty.

Knock at Daisy's door. Tell her I sent you. She will nurture you alongside all the other creatures she takes under her wing.

I will find you there, in one form or another. Together, we will seek shelter from the raging storms beyond her gate.

Know always that I will love you forever, wherever you may be, my darling daughter.

Your adoring father,

Jack

By the time Daisy read the last line, Star was fast asleep. She tucked the blankets around the sleeping child and returned to her bedroom on tiptoes. Sleep was hard to come by with all the questions that raced through her mind.

Chapter 14

PROBING PROVENANCE

The next morning, Emily knew that Charlie would be annoyed even before she left her warm, cozy bed. It was far too early to wake a cat, but not early enough to find Pete Picken before he hit the road. Emily hoped to catch him before he left town in search of antiques. She rushed to dress and left the house just as the sun peeked over the Anglican church steeple. Emily was up and out long before the town began to bustle with morning activity.

She found Pete in his truck at the gas station, pouring over the sports section of the *Journal de Montréal.* When she knocked on the window, he jumped and knocked his hat low over his eyes. He lowered his feet from their perch on the dashboard and rolled down the window.

"What's up with you, out so early in the morning?" Then, reconsidering, he added, "On second thought, let's skip that question and move on to a safer topic."

"Good morning," she sang with exaggerated cheeriness.

"What's so good about it?"

"I'm here. Isn't that good enough?"

"What's so good about that?" he said without raising his eyes from the page.

In a gesture of friendship, Emily put her hand on his arm.

"Don't touch me unless you love me," he said. "And if you love me, buy me something."

"I'll buy you a cup of coffee at Country Kitchen," she offered.

"No, thanks. They're not open yet."

"How about breakfast?"

"No."

"A muffin?"

"No. I cannot be bought."

"A lemon square?" Emily offered.

"No."

"I know," she said. "A butter tart."

"No, no, and no."

"Aw, Pete, don't be like that."

He put down his paper and directed a deadpan stare at her face. "What about *no* don't you understand?"

"You haven't even asked me what I'm doing here at this ungodly hour."

"I repeat: No, no, and no."

"Aren't you going to invite me into your office?"

Pete shrugged. "Climb in. The door ain't locked."

Emily crossed in front of the truck and heaved the door open with a clunk. She scrambled onto the running boards and reached for the handle to hoist herself into the passenger seat. At first, she sat erect, gazing around the parking lot and surveying her surroundings from an elevated point of view.

"Isn't it warm and toasty in here, considering this chilly morning?"

Having returned to reading his paper, Pete merely nodded. She waited a few moments in silence. Still, he perused the sports statistics as if he had forgotten she was there. Her patience began to wane.

"Pete?"

"The answer is no. Now, what's the question?"

"Don't you want to know why I'm here?"

"We already discussed that question. Let's move on. Do you want a cup of coffee?"

"That would be nice," she said in the sweetest, meekest manner she could muster.

Pete put his paper on the dashboard and climbed out of the truck. He had a way of walking with his shoulders hunched and a swing to his step that exuded purpose and confidence. Emily settled happily into the cushioned seat like a queen on her throne. She loved the smell of Pete's truck. She tried to define the various odours. *Pipe smoke mingled with the essence of gas, and a touch of must, with just a hint of aftershave cologne.*

Pete's truck was his storefront when he peddled his wares from shop to shop. Files in a frayed leather briefcase and clipboards of lists cluttered the dashboard. There were remnants of meals on the road: Subway wrappers, Burger King coffee cups and McDonald's hamburger containers littered the floor. The back of the cab was full of curious objects. A box holding a crystal chandelier with brass ring and Tiffany shade perched precariously on top of a brass urn with feet, as well as a stuffed arctic fox with golden, haunted eyes. An oak Diamond Dye cabinet with a tin door painted with laughing children playing Ring around the Rosie balanced on the seat. A footstool with petit-point upholstery snuggled between the slender legs of an upside-down candle stand on the floor behind the driver's seat. Blocking the view through the rear window was a framed map of Upper Canada.

Thinking of these tokens of long-forgotten skills and traditions, Emily immersed herself in reveries. She closed her eyes and tried to imagine what room had flickered in the light of that elegant Tiffany lamp; what hunter had killed that white fox way up in the Canadian north country in the middle of winter; what did the old spinster look like who'd settled her feet on the stool in front of the fire. The mysteries of the past were as fascinating to her as secrets of the present. In Pete's truck, she felt perfectly comfortable in her mental meanderings. She could filter out today's complicated reminders that she, along with everything old, was outdated and useless.

Pete returned with a clatter and a flurry, shattering her contemplation abruptly.

"I think I got it right: half dark roast, half decaf, with one cream and no sugar."

"Exactly. How kind of you to remember."

He rolled his eyes and picked up the paper to resume reading where he had left off.

Emily sipped her coffee, cupping her hands around the warmth of the cup. "I love the smell of your truck."

His response was immediate. "My truck stinks, and it's full of garbage."

Silence settled between them. Soon he reached for his pipe and began filling the bowl, careful not to lose one shred of tobacco. A sweet smell of molasses and rum flavours mingled with the sulphur of freshly lit matches. He tried four strikes and multiple puffs before succeeding in lighting his pipe. Smoke gradually rose from glowing embers of ash and filled the cab. At this point, Emily reassessed her nostalgic fondness for pipes and opened her window for some fresh air.

She knew Pete well enough to know she simply had to wait him out. *When dealing with reluctant subordinates, detectives must perfect patience. Let them think the solution is all their idea.*

Eventually she broached the subject she had in mind. "Pete, didn't you meet that young girl while she was sitting in Daisy's truck yesterday?"

"So?" he said without looking up from his paper, "What of it?"

She waited again, just long enough to pique his interest.

"You wouldn't want any harm to come to the child, would you?"

He folded the paper and set it aside. She gazed vaguely out the window, as if she could not care one way or another.

She asked, "Would you take me down to the Second Concession?"

"I'm busy," he said, reviewing the paper again. When she failed to argue, his curiosity got the better of him. "What's the child got to do with the Second Concession?"

Emily breathed a sigh of relief. *Once you get their attention, do not reveal too many details. You may scare them away.*

"Jack Blossom lives at the end of the Second, down by the Bog. I think we should pay him a little visit, don't you?"

"How do you know where Jack Blossom lives?"

"A little birdie told me." Then with a clever smile, she added, "I have my sources."

"I hate it when you smile like that. Let your sources take you down to the Bog, then."

She resorted to helpless-damsel-in-distress mode. "Pete, you're the only person I can count on to be discreet. This is a very delicate issue. The child's life and safety are at stake, believe me. I think she might be in danger. We cannot wait too long. Someone else may find *her*, before we find *him*."

"What do you mean? What's going on?"

Emily finished her coffee, took the empty cup to the garbage and resettled into her passenger seat. "Let's go find out, shall we? I'll explain on the way."

Chapter 15

AT THE SOURCE

Hunched to one side, Pete drove with one arm draped over the steering wheel. His hat brim cocked to one side, and his kinky hair defied control, tumbling out from under the cap in all directions.

Emily surveyed the scenery as they sped out of town. Her hands folded neatly into her lap, feet barely touching the floor.

"I wonder if people who live on a hill see life differently from those who live in valleys," she said. "When you look out on the world from high up, you have a certain sense of power, of possibility."

The road descended to the west, at the brow of the hill bordered on both sides by cemeteries: Catholics on the south, with graves marked by obelisks and angels; Protestants on the north, with markers dating back to the 1700s. Cedar forests and maple groves clustered at the foot of the first incline, and then freshly planted crops spread like soft green carpets across the flat lowlands.

"When you live down in the lowlands, you can't really see the sun rise or set. You're always behind. At dawn, the clouds turn pink or orange, but the sun actually rises into a blue sky; then, in the evening, the orb disappears behind the hills before the horizon sets on fire."

"I'm on the road before daylight, no matter where I am," said Pete. "As the days get longer, I get up earlier. In summer, I'm at the flea market by three in the morning, driving right into the sun coming up over the horizon."

"I must admit, I rarely see the sunrise myself."

The smooth rhythm of the truck, the purring of the motor and Pete's relaxed manner lulled Emily into a rare mood for honesty.

"Usually, I'm snug in my bed well into the morning. Unless I have a good reason to get up, I hate to disturb the cat. He likes to sleep in. He's very grumpy if he has to leave his cozy bed early."

They crossed the Higginson Creek, overflowing its banks with a broad swath of rippling water. Pete brought the conversation around to more practical topics.

"Farmer Burnside tile-drained his land, but that doesn't do much good when the water level is higher than the land. Sometimes it doesn't pay to plant crops too early."

After turning off the main county road, they headed towards the Bog. Mounds of tree skeletons and uprooted stumps were evidence of clear cutting, where bulldozers and tractors extracted peat from the low-lying wetlands.

"The countryside changes so quickly these days," said Emily with sadness.

"I remember when huge maple trees shaded this road. A person picking blueberries could get lost in the Bog and never come out again."

Pete slowed the truck slightly. Bungalows lined the road, with signs alerting traffic to children playing. Then he sped up again as dwellings gradually became less frequent. Abruptly, the paved road turned to a sandy track. They continued towards the wilder and more desolate wetlands.

"So, why exactly are we going down this deserted road, anyway?" said Pete, finally getting down to the question that had been on his mind since they'd left town. "How did you find out that Jack Blossom lives way out here?"

"Ida, the postmistress, told me the address. We're looking for number 269. I believe it's beyond the sign that indicates a dead-end."

"I discovered that place when I used to go door-to-door, picking antiques years ago. That farm is at the back of nowhere. Why would anyone want to live way out here?"

"Daisy said Jack was a bit of a strange character when he was younger. He was a loner even back then. He returned to the area about a year ago. According to Ida, he came back from Afghanistan, where he'd served with the Canadian armed forces. She read the return addresses on his pension checks. He moved here with his daughter, Aster. I'm hoping we'll find out more by coming down here for a visit."

"For a visit?" Pete snorted defying her to tell him the whole story. "You expect me to believe you're not just snooping?"

"Detectives have to follow where the path leads, Pete," said Emily, quoting from her imaginary *Sleuth Handbook*. "We have a missing person. Where best to start our search than at the source?"

"How do you know he's not just gone for a bit of a holiday?"

"Would you leave your only daughter on her own while you go on vacation?" Detective Emily did not expect him to answer and continued without pausing. "No, there's something omnivorous going on."

Pete deciphered her meaning. "More ominous?"

"That's what I said. Something is screwy. A man just doesn't disappear without warning, leaving a child behind."

A dark sedan sped past them, going the opposite direction. A bald man was at the wheel. His blonde companion stared straight ahead.

"Wasn't that the couple you were talking to in the Country Kitchen?" Emily asked.

"They do look vaguely familiar."

"I wonder what they're doing way out here?"

"They were dressed in city clothes."

"Maybe Jehovah's Witnesses?"

"More like lawyers or undercover cops. Smiling wasn't part of their vocabulary."

The car disappeared in a cloud of dust.

By now, they arrived at the end of the road where the forest encroached from all sides. The numbers of 269 were peeling from a dilapidated mailbox. A faint driveway with grass growing between tire tracks led to a ramshackle log cabin. Signs of activity indicated someone had begun to recover the property from winter's ravages. The freshly mowed lawn glistened in the morning dew. Bedding flowers and plants in pots sat beside the vegetable garden of recently turned black soil. A man's pair of rubber boots stood by the doorstep. A new rope swing hung from the lower branch of an old maple tree in the front yard.

When Pete slowed the truck, Emily's hand was already on the handle.

"Whoa, whoa, Tabernac," Pete said. "Not so fast. What's the plan?"

Emily reached into her pocket and pulled out a pair of cotton gloves. With expertise that only comes with practice, she slipped each slim finger into the gloves, drawing the cotton tight around her arthritic knuckles. She was eager to begin her investigation.

"It doesn't look like anyone's here at the moment."

Pete became increasingly agitated. The volume of his protest raised several decibels. His knuckles were white where his hands gripped the steering wheel, as if he had to hold on tight to resist the temptation to follow her lead.

"Surely you're not going in without permission!"

Emily sucked in her cheeks and ticked her tongue against her teeth, indicating her impatience. Whenever she was on a mission, Pete's voice of reason interfered with her determination.

Detectives must act on impulse, using the element of surprise to discover fresh clues. Delay allows a trail to fade. Throw caution to the wind. Prompt action produces immediate results.

"You stay here." She hoped a voice of calm authority would assuage his fears. "I'll knock on the door. If there's no response, I'll simply try the knob. If I disappear, you keep watch until I get back."

Pete was not convinced. "And if something goes horribly wrong with your plan?"

"We'll deal with that when it happens."

Before he could protest again, she was out of the truck and trotting up the driveway. She could feel his eyes on her back as she knocked. The door creaked open of its own accord. Someone had left in a hurry without pulling the fastener shut. She slipped inside, neatly snapping the latch into place with a click.

Inside, the tiny house was askew; neither doors nor windows were square or level. Hand-hewn beams supported a low ceiling. Sanded pine floors delineated kitchen from living room, with hand-hooked rugs under the kitchen harvest table and in front of the couch. Furniture was sparse. A primitive staircase led to a loft, where Emily presumed were the sleeping quarters.

The personal contents of the home were tidy and neatly arranged for convenience and practicality. Books lined the shelves, all with titles facing outwards. Dishes cluttered the glazed cupboard according to shape and size. Food was safely stowed behind painted cupboard doors. Every article with a practical purpose had its place, as if whoever inhabited the little dwelling took great pride in organization and control.

However, the contents of a desk in the corner of the living room were scattered on the floor. Detached cables snaked on the rug. Emily surmised a computer was missing, along with any memory sticks. Evidence indicated someone had already beaten her to the punch.

Emily could find nothing of interest until she investigated what must have been Jack's upstairs bedroom. The decor was eerily basic: the bed, neatly made without a wrinkle; only a comb and watch on the dresser top; not a book in sight. There were no photos, no pictures on the wall, not even a mirror. An old, scarred fiddle hanging on the wall was the only indication that the inhabitant of the bedroom had ever showed any interest in life.

In a tiny closet under the roof, she found a packet of letters tied with a red ribbon. She slipped them into the inner pocket of her coat.

In a child's room, the stuffed animals were lovingly snuggled in a row on the pillow. Pictures of horses—some cut from magazines, some drawings and some photos—covered the walls. Two photographs were pinned to the mirror. One was a snapshot of a mother and daughter laughing for the camera; the other was a portrait of a soldier in full uniform with medals on his chest. While studying the photos, shivers inadvertently ran up Emily's spine. Both photos had a ghostly quality, as if the smiling people were pretending to be someone they were not. The eyes of the child, especially, were dull and cheerless; the mother's eyes were only dark shadows; the soldier stared blankly towards the lens, as if there were no future, no hope behind his gaze.

The rude honking of Pete's horn startled Emily out of her reveries. She rushed to the window to see two police cars careening down the road towards the little house, leaving plumes of dust in their wake. She stumbled down the stairs and made a beeline for the way she had come in. Then, changing her mind, she ran to the back door of the kitchen and escaped through the barnyard. She detoured around behind the little chicken house and emerged onto the dead-end of the road, as if she had been walking in the Bog below the ridge.

When she emerged, Inspector Allard was already standing beside Pete's truck. She approached, obviously dishevelled, trying to tuck her unruly hair behind her ears and smoothing down her skirts under her overcoat

"Allo, Allard," she said with an exaggerated casual greeting. "What a surprise!"

She could feel her cheeks flushed. She was obviously breathless with unusual exertion. She avoided looking at Pete; she did not need to look to know that he was frowning, with his moustache crowding his pouting upper lip. She could imagine that familiar expression of humiliation and annoyance. Her mind raced through various scenarios, conjuring an explanation for trespassing in this unlikely place.

"What brings you to this deserted neck of the woods?" she said, trying to divert the inspector. She well knew his acumen for guessing the truth.

"I could ask you the same question, Mrs. Blossom. It seems rather strange to find you and Mr. Picken way out here." With a flashlight, Allard glanced over the contents of the extended cab of the truck. Pete always carried an odd assortment of antiques and memorabilia wherever he went. "You wouldn't by any chance be on the hunt for antiques, now, would you?"

"Antiques?" Pete and Emily repeated at the same time.

"You think we're looking for antiques?" Pete said again.

Smiling nervously, Emily acted even more flustered. She pretended guilt, as if caught in the act.

"Now, now, Allard," she said. "We've been friends for a long time. You know I would never do anything even slightly illegal."

Allard straightened himself to his tallest. He puffed out his chest so that his identification label came close to her face. Emily, at four foot ten, stared directly at the brass buttons below his chin.

"Have you ever heard of breaking and entering, Mrs. Blossom? It's a criminal offence, you know!"

Emily heard Pete's breath catch in his throat.

"B and E?"

Allard nodded, his double chin accumulating just above his Adam's apple.

Emily began to chuckle a little, just enough to lighten the atmosphere without insulting the stern constable. She put her hand to her cheek and cocked a glance at him sideways. Then she whispered—softly to appear coy, and exactly loud enough for all the other constables to hear. "Actually, Inspector Allard, I'll let you in on our little secret." She glanced sideways at Pete. Even before she spoke, she knew by his expression that her accomplice was already horrified at whatever explanation she might invent. For added effect, she cupped her hand around her lips as if to prevent anyone nearby from lip reading. "You may think I'm just a little old lady, but nobody says that we don't have …

you know … desires like everyone else." She accentuated the word *desires* as if it were a dirty word.

"Desires?" Allard repeated, not getting her implication.

She giggled, this time with more glee. Pete was experiencing a severe coughing fit.

"Dear Inspector Allard, do I need to spell out the story of the birds and the bees to you, of all people?" She paused just long enough to heighten the suspense. "Pete and I were having a little panky hanky … you know, a little fun in the passenger seat, so to speak. You know what I'm getting at."

At this point, the inspector's face turned bright red, and he began to sputter.

Emily quietly turned with a wiggle to her hips, threw an alluring glance over her shoulder and climbed into Pete's truck as gracefully as possible. Pete turned the key, and the truck roared. They pulled away slowly, leaving the constables clustered around the cruisers. Emily could see Constable Allard in the rear-view mirror, scratching his head and still trying to process what she had told him.

Pete navigated the truck around the circle at the end of the road. He was driving slowly back past the group of police officers when Emily shouted, "Stop!"

He nearly drove into the ditch. "Don't do that!" he yelled back at her.

"Wait. I forgot something."

"There's no way I'm stopping."

Because he was still going quite slowly, Emily simply opened the door and scrambled out of the truck without giving him a chance to speed up. She was already running back towards the cruisers before he slammed on the brakes. She approached one of the uniformed police officers standing by the side of the road, waiting for instructions.

"Aren't you that nice man who loves butter tarts?" said Emily as if she were out for a stroll meeting a friend on the street. "I first met you at the Country Kitchen on the Hill. Perhaps you remember me? Detective Emily Blossom." Before he could answer, she added with a wink, "We're in the same profession, you know."

The constable smiled nervously, glancing over his shoulder to assure himself that Inspector Allard was preoccupied elsewhere.

"Are you here looking for a missing person?" Emily asked casually, hoping to catch the rookie off guard.

"No, Ma'am," he said with a slight accent she could not place. "It's a murder investigation."

"Murder? When? Where?" She tried to keep her voice calm and casual.

"At the magic show on the weekend, a man died under suspicious circumstances. They think the victim lived here. That's all I can tell you."

Emily patted him on the sleeve as if he were an obedient puppy.

"Thank you so much, Officer." She stole a glance at the ID on his uniform. "I believe … Ah, yes, I remember now. Your name is Patterson. Constable Patterson."

He nodded with a surprised smile, pleased that she recognized him personally.

"I will definitely put in a good word for you with Inspector Allard. Have a nice day."

With a quick handshake, she returned to the truck and slipped in beside a scowling Pete Picken. She did not have to see him rolling his eyes at her comment to the constable to know he was annoyed with her games. She knew better than to comment.

Pete sulked while he drove, slumping forward towards the windshield and staring straight ahead. With his hat perched to one side while he puffed on his pipe, he resembled a fuming volcano. She braced herself for the eruption.

"Hanky panky," Pete said under his breath. "Not panky hanky."

Emily's lips quivered ever so slightly into a suggestion of a grin. "What? What's wrong with that?"

"How could you dare suggest we were making out in the truck at the dead end of a deserted road like teenagers?" Pete glared at her from under his hat. "You don't honestly think Allard fell for that one, do you?"

She ruffled and puffed as tall as she could, considering that her forehead barely cleared the dashboard. "Well, it was the best excuse I could come up with on the spur of the moment," she said. "B and E is a serious offence. I did not want him to think I was actually inside the house, did I? You would be considered an accomplice, aiding and abetting, even if you weren't caught with any suspicious belongings."

"What was Allard doing there, anyway?'

"Would you believe a murder investigation?" she said, wishing that she could lie her way out of the straightforward answer. She knew Pete better than to hide the truth. He could see through her evasions every time.

He slammed on the brakes and came to a skidding halt in the middle of the road. He glared at her with cold steely eyes. "Murder? Whose murder?"

Without looking at him, she scrunched up her face into a quizzical expression that she hoped was distracting.

Emily said, "They were headed for Jack Blossom's, weren't they?"

Pete hit hit his forehead on his arms in despair. "Jesus!"

Emily sat quietly with her fingers interlaced in her lap, without comment. She waited, trying to breathe calmly while staring across the fields. Eventually he put the truck into gear and proceeded into town without further comment.

Chapter 16

LONG NIGHTS MOON

My Dear Little Star, sparkling in the late night sky,

May I tell you now about the cycles of the moon? Are you old enough to gaze at the night sky, to stay up past your bedtime, to look at all those stars above?

Where you live at the top of the world, you will see them all in constellations. The Big Dipper, a Great Bear, pointing his finger at the North Star; Cassiopeia, like a giant *W* high in the sky; the tiny cluster of the Pleiades; Dragon, the fish; Orion's silver belt and his sword, where stars are born.

The patterns of stars never change. They are constant and forever, like my love for you, my sweet daughter.

Your father is the moon. He comes and goes. Sometimes you see him. Sometimes he hides. But he will always return to the night sky.

The moon has many shapes. He appears in many ways. Sometimes he is brilliant with full cheeks aglow, laughing with twinkling eyes. Sometimes the moon is only a tiny sliver in the pale blue morning.

When Mr. Moon is busy elsewhere, thousands of stars come out to play. In joy, the Milky Way throws a halo of sparkling galaxies around the sleeping earth. The clouds dance with the wind. Tree fingers tickle the sky.

Do not be afraid when Mr. Moon disappears. He will always return. You will see him far overhead in the deep black sky, winking and laughing. His smile will be especially for you, his own twinkling, starlit daughter.

Chapter 17

LAWS OF GRAVITY

Daisy began every day with a heavy conscience. She knew she had an odd quirk of character that made her different from other people. She considered herself backwards. Not slow, but contrary. She thought in opposites, rather like a dyslexic in life. Because she did not have enough of her own troubles, she dwelled on the misfortunes of others, the peril of the planet and the destiny of the universe. She honed the art of worry to a fine tip.

She was acutely aware of her good fortune, and she counted her blessings. She slept in a cozy bed. She lived in an ancient and secure house of stone. She had enough money to support herself and her animals. She was free to decide how to spend her day. All these were luxuries she sincerely appreciated.

However, in order to absorb the full extent of her good luck, she perfected the practice of worrying about things over which she had absolutely no control.

Being so intent on her own intensity, Daisy assumed that Aster Blossom was like her. She sensed that the young girl was all too familiar with the sorrows of loss. Therefore, she worried all night that Aster would be worried. Overnight, the cycle of anxiety had magnified into a tumultuous ball of difficult scenarios and tragic outcomes.

She had agonized needlessly, or so it seemed. The child was happy from the moment she woke in the morning, bouncing out of bed and eager to embrace all the lovely surprises that she could discover.

Aster—or Star, as Daisy must now remember to call her—found everything about Blossoms Corners fascinating, from the little dove that cooed as soon as daylight brightened the kitchen to a breakfast cooked on the wood stove, to lifting heavy bales in the barn while doing chores.

The girl was ready and willing to absorb every bit of advice Daisy had to offer.

Precautions were obvious to Daisy, but not to Star.

"Always introduce yourself to any animal you meet for the first time."

"Don't walk up behind a horse without letting them know you are there."

"Close gates behind you. Never run in the barn. Do not raise your voice. Never express fear. Keep breathing."

To Daisy, the reasons were self-evident, but the child was inexperienced around animals and needed guidance. Star was perfectly willing, but she had no idea how to behave.

Daisy explained patiently. "Animals are people too. All creatures on earth deserve the same respect we show to other humans. When you meet a stranger, you introduce yourself: 'Hello, my name is Aster. I'm a nice girl, and I want to be your friend.' That's what you say when you meet an animal for the first time. You speak in body language that they will understand.

"You do not have eyes behind your head. You need warning when someone approaches from behind you, so you won't be startled. It's the same with a horse. Speak to Bella and Alie when you are near them.

"There's no need to shout or scold in anger. Explain what the rules are; they will understand. Mind you, it takes time to learn how to make your message clear."

"Even with Friday?"

"We have one rule: Everyone has to get along."

"What if he chases the cats?"

"Friday has come to understand that cats are enchanted." Daisy's smile nestled in the corners of her lips. "Every time Friday even thinks of chasing a cat, some mysterious object flies through the air and discourages him from being disrespectful."

"A mysterious object? Like what?"

"Oh, a bucket, maybe, or a tin can. Never anything that would actually hurt him, but something that makes a very loud noise. He gets the message."

"Like the white cat when she looks at the doves?"

"Exactly. Cats at Blossoms Corners believe that birds are enchanted with special powers to hurl scary missiles through the air at their predators."

Daisy carried on a running commentary about each of the animals as they worked around the barn. Quasi Modo failed chicken school because he had crooked legs. Llarry the llama was kicked out of the petting zoo for spitting on tourists. Howard, a female Rouen duck, fell in love with her soul mate, Donald, who saved her from a fox. Every creature had its special character and challenges.

The stories wove one into another seamlessly. Time disappeared. The events Daisy remembered could have happened yesterday or years ago. Many of the creatures had long since gone the way of forgotten memories. Snippets of instants became the core of universal experience: loneliness, love, friendship, tragedy, loss—all threads intermingling into a litany of adventure and passage. In Daisy's mind, the animals were as human as people were, and perhaps more so. The barn enveloped Daisy and Star into a haven of wonder.

At one point, Aster became uncomfortable, as if she detected a glimmer of doubt in the carefully constructed ideal of Daisy's world. "Daisy, do you ever hear angry, mean voices telling you nasty things about yourself?"

The question seemed totally out of the blue, but Daisy answered in stride as simply as she could. "No, Aster—Star. The only voices that I hear are all the animals calling for their dinner."

"Nobody tells you're not worthy of living?"

Daisy detected a direction to Aster's questions, so she asked, "Do you know someone who said you're not worthy of living, Honey?"

Aster did not pause to find an answer. "Not me. My mother did. She heard voices that told her she was evil and did not deserve to live. She argued with them, but they always won out."

Daisy took a deep breath before she constructed her reply. "We each have our own self-doubts. Life is not easy. But no one can tell you that you are not worthy of living. The way I see it, each one of us is essential to the existence of the universe. We only have one life to live. Every moment is precious."

Aster seemed satisfied with Daisy's answer. She resumed her cheerful countenance and skipped along beside Daisy as they performed the daily chores. Horses received hay and oats. They filled the sheep mangers, replenished the water buckets and threw grain to the chickens. Each animal had its pen or stall. Fences confined them. As the two of them did the chores, they closed the gates and fastened each latch after every task was finished.

"Do the animals mind being penned up?" asked Star. "Do they ever run away?"

Daisy told the story of when the dove named O Solo Mio flew out of the house up into the trees in the valley. "Freedom is a scary thing for a dove who has no defences," she said. "I was torn. I wanted him to be free to fly, but I knew he would not survive."

"He couldn't find food?" said Star in small, wondering awe.

"The world is a dangerous place for a tiny dove. A hawk would find Solo a tasty little morsel. Winter is long and cold for a dove used to a tropical climate. But really, he would probably have died of loneliness without a friend."

"What did you do?"

"There wasn't much I could do. I cooed and called and hoped he would find his way home."

"Did he?"

"Yes, after the third day, I was on my way to the barn. He flew down and landed on my head. I cried and cried."

"You cried? Why? Weren't you happy?"

"I was so worried, I cried from happiness."

Chapter 18

GOLDEN PEGASUS

The morning flew by. Soon each animal was fed, watered and bedded down in clean straw. The physical work for an elderly woman was demanding. For a child, no amount of energy compensated for a lack of muscle strength. Still they proceeded through each task, slowly and systematically until every detail was complete, down to sweeping the floor and emptying the wheelbarrow.

"Time for a rest," declared Daisy.

They were sitting on a bale of hay in the barn, surrounded by comfortable sounds. Horses munched their breakfast. Friday made a bed in the straw at their feet. The barn cat curled up in Daisy's lap purred loudly. The hay smelled of summer preserved in dried timothy grass, sweet red clover and blossoms of black-eyed Susans and daisies. It was the perfect setting for a down-home, old-fashioned country tale.

"One day I was at a horse auction," Daisy began. Then she reconsidered.

She was silent while meticulously sorting through the bale where they sat for just the right size of dried grass. She tucked the stem into the corner of her mouth and sucked absent-mindedly on the wisp of hay. Aster studied her movements carefully. Then she too selected a stem from the dry hay and tasted its sweetness. She stretched her legs out beside Daisy's, and they lounged against the wall side by side.

Then Daisy resumed with a caveat. "Just because I did something foolish, that doesn't mean it's the right thing to do. You understand that, don't you?"

Star sucked on her stem of hay and nodded, with wide, sincere eyes. "What happened at a horse auction?"

Daisy realized that once begun, a story was like a river: there was no turning back. Therefore, she gave in easily, and they both settled in for a good yarn.

"An auction is where people bring animals they don't want anymore, and where other people go to buy them. The auctioneer sets the price. But you never really know what you're buying, and there are no guarantees.

"The livestock auction is held every Tuesday in a town up the road. The sale takes place in a rickety old barn full of tiny pens filled with every sort of farm animal you can imagine. They start with the poultry: chickens of all shapes and colours, quacking ducks, honking geese, gobbling turkeys. Sometimes they even have brilliant feathered pheasants or quail. They cage the fowl in boxes with wire windows so you can peek inside and see sad, scared birds staring back at you with beady eyes. The farm animals, beef cows, goats and sheep are sold at night, so the farmers can attend the sale after evening chores. Sometimes the auctioneer goes until two or three in the morning.

"The horse sale is always in the afternoon. My friend Pete Picken and I used to go to the auction just to see what was happening on the underside of the horse world. You would see the worst cases of disease and injury. Going to a horse auction is a good way to learn, but it's not fun. As gentle or as wild as they are, horses are always magnificent. Humans mistreat them in ways you cannot even imagine."

"Can anyone buy a horse at the sale barn?"

"Any money is good enough. You just have to put in the highest bid."

"How do you know how much to pay?"

"Now, hold on there, little one. Let me tell the story in my own good time. You make me lose my place."

"You and Pete were friends?"

Daisy looked quizzically at the child beside her.

"How do you know Pete Picken?"

"While I was sitting in the truck waiting for you, isn't that the man who brought me some hot chocolate from the restaurant yesterday?"

Daisy pondered the child's answer for a moment before she continued. Pete had a way of getting around town that continually baffled her. She selected another wisp of hay to chew on.

Star interrupted her train of thought. "What happened next?"

"Now, where was I?"

"You and Pete were at the horse auction."

"Oh, yes. That day, I remember, the pens were all full. There were even horses in the far shed. There were draft horses and ponies, mules and burros. They were all sizes, colours and breeds—mares with foals at heel, colts and fillies. They tied the stallions to posts, one next to the other. You can imagine the squealing and kicking that went on.

"You had to be real careful wandering around. The aisles between the pens were barely wide enough for one horse to pass through. When the man unloaded a new bunch from the trailers outside, they'd bring three or four at a time through the dark, narrow passageways. No one cared who was in the way. People had to climb on the fences to get out of the way. Kids, screaming mothers, old farmers with canes—everyone had to jump out of the way or get run over.

"At a place like that, you learn to recognize common horse injuries. Though the beasts seem so big and powerful, horses are actually very delicate. You see foundered ponies with their hooves curled up at the toe; horses with injured knees and capped hocks; breathing problems called heaves, where they suck in at the flanks trying to get air. Some are blind. Some are so skinny you can see every rib. Some are wind suckers; you see them cribbing with their teeth on the fences.

"Hang around at a horse auction, and you'll see it all. That's how you accumulate knowledge. You develop an eye for a good horse, and you learn to recognize problems you can't fix."

"How do you pick out the good ones?"

"A bit of intuition and a lot of experience, but mostly just plain luck."

"Did you see one that day?"

"Hold on, I'm getting there. Now, where was I?"

"Were there any good ones there that day?"

"Oh, yes—that's where I left off. We wandered around for a while, and then Pete went for a smoke. I was in a daze with all the noise and stink of the place. When horses are afraid and panic, they sweat and pee and pooh a lot. My head was spinning. I had to find a quiet place to rest, so I headed for the back stalls. That's when I saw her: the most beautiful horse I ever set eyes on. It was probably because I couldn't see really well in the dark, but the instant I caught sight of her in the shadows, I felt the breath leave my lungs, and my heart flipped."

Daisy paused and looked at the child's face. "You're probably too young to know what true love feels like."

"Gobsmacked," said Aster.

"Pardon me?"

"That's what kids say when that happens. You're gobsmacked."

Daisy furrowed her brow. "Well, if you say so. Somehow that wouldn't be the way I would describe it, but if it works for you … Where was I again?"

"What did she look like?"

"She was a mare, not big, but with a presence larger than all outdoors. She was cream coloured with golden dapples all over her body. She had a flowing mane, and her tail was so long it touched the ground."

Daisy paused, recalling the image in her mind's eye.

"The most striking feature was her eyes. That mare had golden eyes that flashed like fire, even in the darkest corner of that dingy barn. There was something exceptional about her. She was so regal, so elegant, as if even in the worst conditions, she would never surrender her wild, free spirit.

"I approached her stall and whispered, 'Hey, girl. You're all right. Don't be afraid.'

"I put my hand out, and she sniffed my fingers with flaring nostrils. I waited. You have to be patient when you meet a new horse. After a moment, she sensed I didn't mean any harm. She came closer, and I could feel her breath on my cheek. That's how horses blow kisses."

Daisy remembered whom she was talking to, and she altered the tone of her voice.

"Mind you, I was taking a chance. You can get badly bitten if a horse doesn't trust you."

"Did she bite you?"

"No, that horse didn't have a mean bone in her body. At that point, she didn't have a friend in the world."

"Then what happened?"

"I went to find Pete. I told him about the mare, and he came with me to check her out. We both thought she was pretty extraordinary.

"But then reality set in. It was late, and I had to get back to chores. More important, though, I didn't have much money on me. Pete knew the auctioneer. He went to talk to him, to see if we could leave a bid. The guy laughed when we told him how much we were willing to pay. 'You'll never get her for that price,' he said. 'Well,' said Pete—he was much calmer about the whole thing than I was, so I let him do the talking—'That's our price. If she goes for more, sell her to the highest bidder. That's the best we can do.'

"As we walked back to the truck, I remember saying, 'It's worth taking a chance. I'd never forgive myself if I didn't even try to save that horse from that place.'"

"What did Pete say?"

"He agreed with me. We didn't say much more on the way home. He left me off at the farm, and that was that."

"That was that?"

"Well, I figured I'd never see the mare again. I knew my bid wasn't very high, but I didn't have any more money to spend on a horse I didn't need. I decided that I had had a fine adventure, that I'd learned a lot and that it was time to get on with practical life, instead of dreaming about horses all the time."

"That's the end of the story?"

"No, actually. It was just the beginning. A few days later, Pete was down for a visit. We were standing outside the barn chatting when I saw a truck and a horse trailer coming down the road. I didn't think much about it because some days we have a lot of traffic going by. The next thing I knew, the truck pulled into the driveway. A guy got out and walked up to Pete as if they knew each other. Then they walked around to the back of the trailer, and out came that beautiful mare. She was just as glorious as I remembered. Pete handed me the lead rope, and I was flabbergasted. I didn't know what to say and broke down in tears."

"You were happy?"

"Yes. I couldn't believe it. She turned out to be a wonderful horse. We had her for years."

"Could you ride her?"

"Oh, yes. Actually, Pete was the first one to try her out. He just jumped right up onto her back, and she didn't do a thing. I thought he was crazy. Nobody does that with a horse he doesn't know."

"Pete did."

"Yes, he did. I didn't even know he knew how to ride a horse."

"Was she fun to ride?"

"Yes, but she didn't like giving riding lessons very much. She did it, but it wasn't her favourite activity. Mostly she loved having babies. She gave us seven foals: three blacks, two palominos, and one cremello—a white horse with blue eyes. The last one was a golden mare with a black mane and tail who loved to gallop circles around her mother."

"What happened to her?"

Daisy caught her breath before she finished the story. She realized she couldn't hide the truth, but she worried that Star would find the ending too sad. However, there was no way around the facts of life on a farm.

"One night there was a terrible storm. Crashes of lightning and thunder came right over the farmhouse. The horses were out to pasture, and they won't come into the barn on stormy nights. They turn their backs to the wind, standing huddled and still, until it's all over. In the morning, the golden horse had been struck by lightning. She was lying in the mud and could not get up. All the others were safe. When a horse cannot run free, she will not live long. We buried her up on the brow of the hill, so she could be with the herd while they graze in the sunshine. Sometimes I think I see her galloping along the ridge with her mane and tail flying in the wind."

When Daisy finished her story, they sat for a while longer. They listened to the muffled sounds of horses chewing and cat purring.

Star was the one to break the silence between them. "My mother had golden eyes," she said.

Chapter 19

LOVE LETTERS IN THE SANDS OF TIME

Emily was standing on the curb as Pete drove away. Then she saw the curtains move in her living room window. She put the key in the door lock, knowing someone would be anxiously awaiting her arrival.

Sure enough, a wail of complaints greeted her as soon as she stepped into the hallway.

"I know, I know, Charlie. I left you alone all morning. You haven't had a snippet of company. Your stomach is empty, and you're about to roll over and expire from starvation as we speak."

The cat apparently revived enough to leap around in circles, meowing loudly. His tail waved in fluffy exuberance, and his double claws clicked on the floor. As soon as Emily stepped into the room, he stretched his long body as high as he could. Yowling and scolding, he embedded his claws into her pants leg. She reached down and scratched him behind the ears while gently extracting the fabric of her trousers from his sharp nails.

"I know. You make yourself very clear. I feel terrible leaving you all alone to your own devices. I'll make it up to you. I have some tasty treats saved for special occasions." When addressing her cat, Emily adopted a manner of speaking that combined childlike intonation with a lilting hum. She reserved this tone of voice exclusively for speaking to her pet. "We'll have a tea party. I'll have a lovely cup of tea. You will have cattykins."

After hanging her coat and purse on a hook in the hall, Emily proceeded quickly to the kitchen. She carried on a running commentary as she went about the ritual of preparing tea. "We both deserve to pamper ourselves after surviving such terrible trails and tributations." In her mind, she heard Pete's voice chiding her, so she corrected her misspoken phrase in a soft whisper. "I should say, trials and tribulations."

Then she continued bustling around the kitchen.

"First we select the proper cup for such an ostentatious occasion; the one with blue forget-me-nots and violets will suit nicely. Next, the tea. How about lavender mint with a touch of Lady Grey? For you, young man, we'll try liver pâté with caviar as an appetizer. On second thought, you may find the caviar a bit too salty, and the fish eggs will stick in your teeth. We'll try confit de canard instead. This silver tray will suit our little banquet nicely. We have a veritable feast."

Emily gathered up all the utensils and ingredients for their meal and carried everything into the living room. She placed the tray on a candle stand next to her wing-backed armchair. Charlie eagerly waited by her chair for his portion of the meal.

Over the years, she had handpicked her furniture to create the appearance of Victorian elegance mixed with cozy intimacy. The slant top desk in the corner featured elaborate flower patterns inlaid in mahogany. A tiffany lamp with stained glass shade sat on a washstand, decorated with hand-carved handles and delicate brass escutcheons. An oriental rug added to the warmth of the room shaded by velvet drapes.

As an art connoisseur, Emily collected works by early Canadian artists. Her paintings had become quite valuable over the years. Landscapes in oils included scenes of quaint Quebecois villages, broad-brush strokes of autumn maples on the East Coast and mountain ranges of the Far North.

At an auction recently, she had bought an eerie landscape in oils. The painting in its original frame was by a British artist dated 1916. The sunset scene appealed to Emily's imagination, particularly when she realized the artist had painted the work near the end of the First World War. The artist used an ominous pastel palette of light reflecting on snow with purple forests and a dark village in the valley below. Emily mused how J. Tyndall Midgely was feeling as he painted with cold fingers, knowing that countless men were dying in the trenches not far from home. Tragedy appealed to her slightly morbid sense of life's fragility. She hung the painting on a prominent wall opposite an east facing window. When she sat in her wing chair, she studied the scene as the light changed outside.

She placed a porcelain saucer filled with pâté and confit on the floor beside the cat. Then she settled into her favourite chair and sipped her tea to determine whether it had properly steeped.

When the spinster and the cat had devoured their feast, Emily got down to business of her alter identity as a sleuth. She thought of Jack Blossom, when he served in the army on the other side of the world in Afghanistan. Now he was dead.

From her coat pocket, she retrieved the packet of letters she had recovered from Jack Blossom's bedroom.

"Now it's time for Detective Emily Blossom to get back down to work," she said to Charlie, who had already curled up on his favourite cushion for a well-deserved after-dinner snooze.

Detectives must pay special attention to the details of a case. One must thoroughly delve into the background of the parties involved. In most cases, the victim has met his assailant at some time in the past. All forms of correspondence are useful in conducting a comprehensive investigation.

To avoid damaging the evidence, she very carefully unfolded the package of fragile papers tied with a red satin ribbon.

The first pages were poems written on parchment paper frayed at the edges and torn at the creases. Each one was dated and signed by Carly MacLeod.

Gathering Flowers

While gathering flowers in the spring,
Buttercups and violets,
Thoughts float on soft breezes
Like butterflies,
Reminding me
Of gentle friends,
And you.

Love

On a blade of spring grass,
You are the sparkle of dew.
On a hot summer's day,
You are the breath of soft breeze.
On a crisp autumn eve,
You are the crackle of fallen leaves.
On my rosy cheeks in winter,
You are a gentle flake of snow.
You are my hope,
My dream,
My inspiration.
You are my love.

When Do I Love You?

I love you in the sunshine.
I love you in the rain.
I love you through the laughter.
I love you through the pain.
I love you in the evening,
When the stars begin to shine.
I love you when I'm happy.
I love you all the time.

Emily paused in her reading and sighed. "Young love, Charlie, is so simple and straightforward."

The next pages were slips of paper torn from a notebook. Each message was folded several times and crumpled, as if handled surreptitiously from a closed palm. Emily guessed these were notes passed along during class time. One note read, "Meet me behind the school at recess out by the big tree. Love, Carly."

Another one said, "Jack, Frankie's skipping history class to go for a smoke. Want to come with?"

The third note was three simple words: "I missed you."

"I guess Jack didn't show up for the smoke break," Emily said to her cat.

As she shuffled through the notes, the next poem appeared to have been prepared as a school assignment.

The Scarlet Cardinal
by Carly MacLeod

Proud Mr. Cardinal,
High up in the trees,
Flashing his colours
So all the girls see.
How handsome he is;
How pretty he sings.
He thinks he's quite special
Before he takes wing.
He flies through the air,
So valiant, so free.
He's full of himself;
He cares not for me.

Teacher's Comments: Clever attempts at rhyme. Punctuation inconsistent. Good appreciation for the form of poetry as expression of emotion. B+

Scrawled on scraps of lined loose-leaf sheets torn from a spiral notebook were the following notes.

Dear Jack,

Please don't be mad. Frankie will fiddle for me at the championships.

Frankie said if I won't let him play for my step dance competition, he'll never speak to me again. He says he's as good as you are.

I hope you won't mind.

You are the one I love.

Love, Carly

Dear Jack,

I'm sorry I lied to you. I will never do it again. Call me as soon as you get this.

C

Dear Jack,

Frankie and I are engaged. Will you come to our wedding?

Your friend, Carly

"Poor Jack," Emily said.

Charlie slept on. The sound of gentle purring and the clicking of her grandfather clock reminded Emily of time passing. She sat quietly with the letters in her lap. She mused on the significance of a few lines scrawled on scraps of paper. Memories stored away for so many years as remnants of young lives tumbling through time, innocent of the whims of destiny.

How fascinating that we can enter into other people's lives so briefly noted and feel as though we know these strangers intimately.

Dated years later, the next letter was typewritten, addressed to Corporal Jack Blossom, Canadian Armed Forces, Kandahar, Afghanistan.

Dear Jack,

I heard you were coming home on leave. It's hard to believe you have been away so long.

Things didn't work out for me and Frankie.

He treated me so badly. You can't imagine how mean he was to me. When he threw me down the stairs, I finally realized he was really dangerous. I haven't seen him since he enlisted in the forces, like you did.

Please get in touch with me when you come home. I'd love to see you again.

Love,

Carly

The next letter was a printed copy of an e-mail.

Dear Jack,

I don't know how to tell you this. You're so far away, so I'll make it simple. I'm pregnant. The baby is due in six months. Please come home.

Carly.

The next e-mail message was only one line.

Dear Jack,

Please send money.

Carly

"Oh dear, oh dear," Emily said. "How much is written in a few short lines. Life does have its twists and turns. That's enough research for now."

Emily carefully folded the letters back into their neat bundle and tied the ribbon back into place. The packet seemed smaller than when she had begun to read the notes; however, she let the thought slip away. She did not notice that one letter was missing.

She stored the letters in the table drawer and carried the tea party dishes to the kitchen.

"I'm glad to get down to something practical like washing dishes. Even housework is a relief when one wants to avoid too much thinking."

Chapter 20

MUSIC OF THE SPHERES

If Emily wanted to know more about local fiddle competitions, she knew she would have to attend the Strawberry Social at the Orange Lodge Hall at McInness Crossing. The old-timers would all be there, as well as youngsters who still carried on the music and dance traditions handed down from their elders through the generations.

Angus McInness organized the event in order to raise money to restore the old dance hall. In the old days, weekly square dances used to be the entertainment for the locals, young and old alike, before TV and movies. In Scottsdale, descendants of Scottish immigrants preserved the fiddle tunes and step dances passed on from the early settlers of Upper Canada. Families of all ages gathered at the hall to dance a few waltzes, jigs and reels, in celebration of the arrival of spring and strawberries, the first ripe fruit of the season.

Emily was at a bit of a loss as to how to get to McInness. She knew Pete had had enough of her shenanigans. Daisy was preoccupied with the child. She was not enthusiastic about asking any of the old-time fiddlers for a lift in case she decided to leave early. The easiest option, but not the most sensible, was to hitchhike.

She consulted Charlie. "Either no one will pick me up because they think I'm a crazy old lady, or someone will take pity on my fragility and give me a lift. What have I got to lose?" Her cat made no comment. "Silence gives consent. That settles it."

She chose a comfortable pair of warm slacks and a bright dressy top. "That way I'll be casual and fancy at the same time. I'm glad it's not cold or rainy tonight. My wool coat and ankle boots should suit quite nicely with a bright satin scarf. Let's not forget a flashlight."

Thus equipped, Emily headed to the highway leading south out of town. McInness was the next village down the road, so she did not think a lift would be too difficult to come by.

Sure enough, the third car to pass slowed and backed up. A cheerful young woman greeted her and invited her into the passenger seat.

"Thank you so much, my dear," said Emily. "How nice you are to pick me up. I'm only going down the road to McInness."

"No problem. That's on my way."

After they drove for a few moments, the driver asked Emily if she was afraid to hitchhike.

"Who would want to harm a little old lady like me?" Emily answered. "If I'm thumbing a ride, I haven't got anything of value. I'm not exactly sexually appealing. Actually, I've learned over the years that the older you are, the more you become invisible. Nobody cares about you anymore. There are a lot of advantages to being overlooked."

"I hope you never find out any different," said her companion. "As I face old age, I have something to look forward to, then?"

"Oh yes, my dear. Life has all kinds of surprises in store for you. I feel so lucky to have lived this long. A person is never too old to learn new things. Now, here we are. Thank you so much for the lift."

"Have a nice evening. Don't wear out your dancing shoes."

"I have no intention of doing that, you can be sure. I outgrew my Cinderella slippers long ago."

Emily watched as the tail lights disappeared down the road before she turned to enter the brightly lit hall. The room was already full of people, and the din of excitement and cheer was almost tangible.

Emily paid her entrance fee and purchased a ticket for the fifty-fifty draw.

"I hope you win," said the youngster selling the tickets.

"I bet you say that to everyone."

"Only the pretty ones," he said with a wink.

Emily blushed in spite of herself. She loved compliments from young men, even though she knew they were only teasing. *A detective should never be above a little flirtation. You can never tell who can provide useful information when it comes to investigating murder. Everyone is a potential source. Besides, you need all the friends you can get.*

Entering the hall was like stepping back in time. The decor was simple and practical. The walls of tongue-in-groove panelling were the colour of soft natural wood. A simple chair moulding ran the length of the building. Three tall windows along both sides admitted light and air into the vast, noisy room. Sky blue mouldings highlighted geometric diamonds and squares patterning the ochre ceiling. Plain hardwood floors creaked and rippled under the weight of the milling crowd. Benches lined the walls where the audience vied for seats when the entertainment began.

Mothers minded small children. Little girls with ribbons in their curly locks wore bright-coloured party dresses and patent leather shoes with lace socks. Boys, clad in jeans with broad cuffs, plaid shirts and suspenders, parted their hair on the side and slicked it into place with shiny gel. They played tag, using their sassy little sisters as interference.

Matrons with tightly permed silver hair huddled in knots, gossiping about their neighbours; they threw glances over their shoulders as if spreading secrets into the air. The men with bellies that amply overlapped their trousers hitched their hands on hips and watched the activities with detached humour. Locals who attended such gatherings were out for a good time, chattering like sparrows on a sunny day.

Angus McInness stood above the crowd with the imposing stature of a kindly benefactor. As the host and organizer, he could silence the roar of the crowd merely by raising his hands above his head. He did not need to raise his voice to be heard. His distinct bellow echoed clearly into every corner of the hall. "Welcome to everyone on this fine spring evening. We have come together this evening to enjoy good music and good company. Some of the finest fiddlers in the region join us right here tonight, folks. Anyone who wants to perform should see me to get on the list.

"This old hall has seen many grand parties and get-togethers. If only the walls could talk, they would be witness to some mighty fine traditions. The money we raise this evening will go towards repairs and maintenance of the building and grounds. Thank you all for coming out this evening. Have a great time. Enjoy yourselves, and we'll see you here next year—same time, same place, God willing."

With that greeting, Angus left the stage, and the Scottsdale Old Time Fiddlers launched into a lively jig.

Performers in their turn emerged from the throng of revellers when the Master of Ceremonies called out their names. They entered and exited the rustic stage at the far end from two steep sets of stairs with banisters. Dancers dipped and bowed like bubbles floating in an eddy of swirls, while the music intermingled with the conversations and greetings. The crowd on the floor made way for dancers of all ages. Couples swayed and dipped to familiar waltzes, each with unique style and grace honed over years of practice. Little children learned steps from smiling adults, who were holding tiny hands and exaggerating the rhythms and movements to the flow of the music.

Emily was in her element, mesmerized by the myriad interactions between people. She considered herself a virtual stranger to this colloquial gathering of friends and families. She enjoyed people-watching in the belief that she was an outsider, a voyeur.

She heard snatches of conversations, and she witnessed winks, glances and expressions that spoke an infinite variety of experiences. Tender glances between young lovers, stolen hugs between couples intertwined through years of togetherness, angry scowls of disapproval from a parent, a questioning cock of the head from an impudent child—all gestures were fodder for Emily's fertile imaginative mind.

A good detective hones the art of astute observation. Practice is the key to seeing what is underneath the surface of human nature.

The resonant voice of Angus McInness startled her when he spoke so near that she could feel his breath on her cheek. People had to speak loudly and lean in close to one another in order to carry on a conversation in spite of the clamour. When Angus interrupted her study of human behaviour, he was the last person she guessed would approach her. In these surroundings, she considered him a celebrity. She was nobody of significance. Of all people, why would he go out of his way to speak to her?

"Mrs. Blossom? I don't believe we've met," he said, extending his giant hand in welcome. "My wife, Bessie, pointed you out. How nice that you've come to support our event. We're always glad to see new faces."

"I've lived in Emerald Hill for several years now." Emily was embarrassed to admit how long she had actually lived in the area without attending such an important social occasion. "I thought it was high time I attended one of your fund raising efforts. I'm so glad I did.

I'm impressed at the attendance. How fine it is that so many people come out to participate!"

Angus stood above her, so close that she felt his presence like a hovering shadow, enveloping her. She sensed he had ulterior motives.

Bessie, with the practice of an experienced know-it-all, watched them from across the room. She was a heavyset person, not tall, but energetic and strong willed. With an expression of urgency, she was signalling to her husband to proceed with the conversation. She made a thumbs-up gesture that indicated to Detective Blossom one of two things: either she was happy with his progress (which Emily doubted), or she wanted him to continue the discussion upstairs.

The investigator took her cue from the situation. She decided to come to the point rather than pretend to find excuses for her presence. "Actually, Mr. McInness, I did come here tonight especially to meet you. I wonder if there is somewhere we could go to talk in private?"

Her host jumped at her suggestion. He pushed the crowd aside and made way for her to follow. He held her arm as he escorted her to the back stairway. Heads turned, briefly curious, but no one seemed to pay much attention to their escape from the throngs.

Upstairs was a small kitchen and meeting hall. Memorabilia of the Orange Lodge decorated the room. Relics of symbolic rituals, mallets for restoring order during meetings, embroidered tapestries and oil lamps dated back more than one hundred years. Glass-fronted cabinets contained leather-bound books on the history of the lodge, and photographs of past presidents hung on the walls. Compared to the din below, the room was quiet, like dust.

Angus spoke nervously at first. "So, Mrs. Blossom, why are you really here? My wife noticed you as soon as you came into the hall. She says you would never show up here unless you were investigating a crime."

His abrupt manner took Emily aback. As a detective, she'd intended to do the interrogation. His formality had fooled her. Initially, she'd thought her host was a bit reticent and retiring, that he used his stage presence as a bluff to cover for shyness. She realized she had entirely misread the man. He was a strong force with whom to reckon.

"My wife says you are a detective. You have a reputation for solving mysterious deaths in the area. We are guessing that you have come because of the passing of Jack Blossom."

Angus placed an uncomfortable, straight-backed, antique armchair for Emily. He stood over her beside a table that served as a desk. However, she remained standing; she could think better on her feet. She hardly knew where to begin, and she began to pace.

"Mr McInness ..."

"Call me Angus."

"Well, then, let's begin again. My name is Emily. I also go by the name of Detective Blossom. You have caught me off guard. I did come to ask for information about Jack Blossom, but I did not know that news of his death had become public knowledge."

To illicit reliable information from a source, detectives must remain calm and neutral. Never show surprise or astonishment.

Emily continued in an even, expressionless tone. "I wonder if you knew the lad when he was younger. I'm interested in his background. My concern is really about the welfare of his daughter."

Now it was Angus's turn to be surprised. "I didn't know he had any children," he said. "I didn't even realize he was married."

"Married? Maybe not. However, I believe he did have at least one child. Perhaps you knew Jack long before that, when he was a fiddler in his teenage years. Were you involved with the fiddle and step competitions back then? Did you know him as a young lad?"

Angus relaxed his shoulders, sat down in a chair, crossed his legs and settled in for a chat. He indicated the chair he had placed beside him. "Please do sit down Mrs. Blossom—Emily. I can tell you what you want to know. I've been fiddling all my life, like my father and his father before him. I know all the young people who have taken up playing since I was a youngster myself. I knew Jack well and was one of his teachers."

Emily allowed herself to sit down. She was feeling more in her element once she realized that Angus McInness was a storyteller at heart. He was a keeper of lore. Music preserved the traditions of his people; stories brought their heritage to life. She had come to the right source.

Angus began his narrative without prompting. He needed little encouragement to talk about his passion for Celtic arts.

"Young Jack Blossom was one of the most talented musicians I've ever come across in all my years of playing tunes. He had a natural gift, as if all the generations of fiddle players back in the old country passed on their talents through his blood and their genes. Some people have a natural, innate ability to play, like they were born with a violin in their hands. However, not all of them are willing to put in the hard work and practice to become really good. Jack was willing to work hard, to study and to practice for hours on end. He got to the point where he could play better than fiddlers who were a lot older than he was, even those who might have had more talent than he did. What he didn't come by naturally, he taught himself by rote. He played scales and arpeggios by the hour. Most young people don't have time for the drudgery of learning keys, notes and time signatures; all they want to do is get up there and play tunes. That only works so far. You need to have the theory and muscle memory to carry you past the point of concentration. When the music takes over, you have to be able to follow it without thinking.

Only then does your whole being become a part of the sound you create. That's what cuts the good ones out of the flock. The champions work hard to get to the top."

"I think it must be a very difficult instrument to play," said Emily. "It's not like a guitar or a piano. There are no frets to indicate where the notes are."

"The fiddle is finicky, like a temperamental female. I don't mean to offend—Bessie tells me to be politically correct, but you can't change a man's nature. A violin is very unforgiving. If you don't place your finger exactly on the right place on the string, you produce a god-awful sound so out of tune that your ears ache. If you don't pull the bow with exactly the correct pressure, the squeak you produce will force your listeners out of the room. Some people practice years only bowing, never mind the fingers on the notes, just to learn how to produce a harmonious sound from one end of the stroke to the other. I haven't even mentioned the rhythm of the tunes. People have to be able to dance to the music. It's not about producing harmony that an audience can appreciate. When a good fiddler picks up his instrument, nobody just listens—you have to get up and dance, and it's impossible to sit still. When you hear the good ones, the fingers and the body talk to one another without words. The brain gets out of the way. If you have to think about what you're doing, it's too late; the tune is way out there ahead of you, and you're left behind before you even get started."

"What's the difference between a violin and a fiddle?"

"Basically, they're the same instrument. Context is the definition. Violins are for classical musicians. The clarity and purity of the sound demand extreme skill and control over the details.

"Everyone can play the fiddle. Life is for living, fiddles are for dancing and perfection is irrelevant. A fiddle is alive, as quirky and unpredictable as life itself. If you make a mistake, you have style. If you hit the wrong note, you're playing harmony. If you trip on the notes, pick yourself up and keep going to catch up. There's no such thing as right and wrong. Just play, and you'll figure it out."

Emily sensed her host could talk forever about the traditions and the art of fiddling. However, she needed to bring the topic back around to her investigation. "Tell me more about Jack. Did he have a friend called Frankie?"

"Frankie Duval. There was another case. You know the French: They're all hot-headed. Frankie was a scrapper."

"They hung around together?"

"You know how kids are. Jack and Frankie were best pals. They did everything together. Bessie used to say, 'If they didn't have each other to compete with, neither one would be any good.' In some ways, she was right. Of the two, Jack was the better player. He had better technique and more control over the details. Frankie was out for the fun of it, but he was one helluva fiddler. He could make up the tunes on the fly. If he got in trouble, he could scale his way out. Jack had to practice harder. That's why he was better in the competitions. The judges could measure his style against a chart of standards. Jack knew the traditional tunes, and he would put his own spin on the familiar jigs and reels. Frankie was more dramatic. He could play a waltz that would send shivers up and down your spine, but he didn't have the same polish. They'd always try to outdo each other. Some kids are very competitive."

Angus paused, lost in reverie. Then he continued without prompting.

"Fiddle kids have a game. One of them fingers the strings, and the other wraps his arm around from behind and does the bowing. Jack and Frankie would switch places fingering and bowing and never miss a beat.

"Jack was always composing tunes. He wrote a reel called 'The Dove and Falcon Reel.' He and Frankie would play two falcons spiralling up and down the scale, with little sound effects and fancy bowing to portray a dove cooing in between the measures. The reel was one of the most popular amongst the kids. Carly would get to step dancing for the two boys, and there was no stopping her feet flying so fast. They'd start out slow, and the tune would pick up speed as they got going. They were all really talented. Good, wholesome fun—that's what the kids did for amusement in those days, not like today where they all have those darn cell phones and don't even talk to each other face-to-face anymore."

Angus's eyes twinkled as he searched his memory for his favourite tales about the good old days.

"One summer night, we had a great dance going on here. The fiddlers were on fire. Jack and Frankie were playing together, and Stella was on the keyboard. I remember it like it was yesterday. It was so hot that we had all the doors and windows open. Everybody was reeling and jigging and dancing as if there was no tomorrow. Every so often, Jack would hoot, and Frankie would holler just to get the dancers revved up. At one point, the two boys got up off their stools, kept playing, went out the back door, moved around past the open windows and came in again at the front. Nobody even knew they were gone. The crowd just kept on stepping and jumping. None of them missed a beat."

"Did something happen between the two boys?" asked Emily. "Jack left home when he was still quite young, didn't he?"

"You know how lads are. They reach a certain age, and then lassies get in the way. Those two were no different. Carly MacLeod was a pretty redhead—bright, smart and sassy. She took a shine to both the boys and challenged one against the other. Bessie said she was trouble, and Bessie's always right. Carly was a step dancer. She was very athletic and strong, one of those hardy Scottish girls with muscled thighs, big-chested so she could dance forever without losing her breath.

"When a dancer performs, she's right out there in front of the judges, with a smile you can see from a mile away. Truth be told, she relies completely on her fiddler to keep her in step. Not only does the fiddler have to be able to set the beat, but he also has to be able to adjust to the dancer's pace. If she stumbles, he has to make allowances; if she speeds up, he has to stay with her, but he dare not get ahead of her steps. The relationship between dancer and fiddler is very intimate, almost extrasensory. They don't even look at each other. They communicate through the music.

"Carly was always sweet on Jack, but Frankie could play a better accompaniment. When it came to the championship, Carly chose Frank to play for her. That would have been fine, except she had already promised herself to Jack two months before the competition.

"There was a dance the week before the championships. Jack had a shot for first place in his category. Everyone knew Carly had a good chance at winning in her division, but a dancer is only as good as her fiddler. The kids were all hanging around outside in between performances. I was the MC.

"Somebody came running into the hall, shouting that there was a fight outside where the boys had knives. As it turned out, only Frankie had a knife. Carly was standing on the sidelines. She pretended that she had nothing to do with the argument, but we all knew she was the cause of their disagreement. As soon as Jack saw the knife, he had the good sense to back off. He left the hall, and we didn't see him again. He didn't show up for the competition and forfeited his chance at the championship. The next thing I heard, Jack had left the country—'gone travelling' was all he said to his mother. She was devastated. He enlisted in the armed forces shortly after that, as soon as he turned 18."

"What happened to Carly and Frank?"

"Frank was a hothead. He couldn't keep his cool under pressure and didn't place well in the championships for his category. Then when he was supposed to play for Carly, she snipped at him just before going onstage. He packed up his fiddle and left the hall. Carly had to use the house fiddler for her competition."

"Did she win?"

A quirky look passed over Angus's face. Conflicting emotions played across his brow. "You know, I don't even remember. Bessie could tell you. I do know they never played that reel again. The two falcons flew the coop, and the dove's feathers moulted. By that time I was so fed up with those kids that I lost all interest. There were younger ones coming up in the ranks, and I concentrated on them. I know kids have to be kids, but for me, tradition is more important. Love comes and goes, but traditions endure."

Angus glanced at Emily as if he had forgotten she was there. Then he continued pensively. "It's funny, isn't it? As soon as a note sounds, it disappears. Harmony lasts only as long as the vibrations echo in the hall." His eyes teared up. "Yet, music goes on forever."

His words settled amongst the dust in the corners of the old hall. Trails of music floated up the stairs like distant memories.

Eventually, Emily broke the silence between them. "Angus, I have one last question before I let you get back to your guests. I know you are a busy man this evening." She paused, assessing the best way to phrase her next question. "How did you hear of Jack's death so soon?"

Her hesitancy was unnecessary. Angus responded easily. "The grapevine is very efficient, Mrs. Blossom. Word travels quickly in this community. Bessie's sister's daughter is a nurse at the emergency ward of the hospital. She was on duty when the ambulance arrived. I gather the event was quite dramatic."

"In what way?"

"Actually, she's here this evening. You can ask her yourself. I'll introduce you."

"Thank you so much," Emily said, rising from her seat. She extended her hand, which he enveloped into his farmer's grip. She tried not to wince at his hearty handshake. "You have been most helpful, Mr. McInness. And please thank your wife as well. She is very perceptive."

"Nobody had better try to pull one over on Bessie, Detective Blossom," Angus said proudly. "I learned that lesson long ago. She knows the news around the countryside, long before anything ever even happens."

Chapter 21

ROSE MOON

My Star Child,
I remember spring back home in Canada, full of hope and promise.
Flowers poke their heads out of frozen soil, seeking warm sunshine.
The buds on trees begin to swell, bursting with hope and joy.
Mother maples overflow with sap sparkling at the
tips of branches, rushing to meet the day.
The first blades of meadows turn the brown dust of
winter to tender green in one flash of day.
Winter patches of snow shrink towards the corners of forest,
then melt and disappear
into rivulets of sparkling, fresh water,
tumbling, bubbling towards plentiful rivers.
I can smell the crisp fresh air,
hear the first song of a robin.
Soon necklaces of geese will pattern the
powdery skies teasing the clouds.
Love coursed in my veins when you were
but a star spark on the horizon,
as sure and inevitable as the energy that
bursts forth in buds and blossoms
when the trees awake from their long winter sleep.
How I wish I could turn back time,
feel that joy,

play with unfettered abandon,
sing and dance until the early hours of dawn.
How quickly, in an instant, joy can disappear,
like a flame extinguished with one puff of breath,
leaving only a smoky trail of dreams
shattered into scintillating shards of sparkle dust,
scattering like milkweed seeds into the winds of time.
My wish for you, my lovely daughter:
May you experience never-ending joy of pure love
in spring, which makes life worth living.
Your adoring father,
Jack

Chapter 22

DEADLY POISON

Angus introduced Emily to Bonnie MacDonell.

Ms. MacDonell was petite and vibrant. Her eyes were strikingly blue and shining with electric enthusiasm. A quick smile revealed pearly, perfect teeth. She wore a pink cardigan sweater and tight jeans, with a rhinestone belt buckle. Everything about the lass exuded warmth and comfort. Emily thought Bonnie MacDonell would be the perfect nurse: her sparkling effervescence was certain to reassure patients even in the most dire of circumstances.

Somehow, the subject of hitchhiking as Emily's mode of transportation came up in their conversation. Mrs. Blossom suspected that Bessie had already engineered the arrangements in whispers behind her back. Bessie was a capable busybody who made it her business to connect people in useful ways.

"I'm going that way," said Bonnie. "I can give you a lift back to the village. That way we can talk in private."

Emily said her goodbyes and headed back to Emerald Hill in Bonnie's car.

Again, Emily suspected that Bessie had a hand in encouraging Bonnie to cooperate with Detective Blossom's investigation. Bonnie did not take much prodding when Emily asked what had happened at the hospital.

People tend to reveal personal details to detectives quite willingly. With very subtle prompting, a good investigator lets the informant do the talking. A relaxed witness who does not feel under pressure is more likely to provide accurate testimony.

"Actually, I'm glad to talk about the incident."

Once Bonnie began to talk, Emily listened with rapt attention.

"The whole affair took us all by surprise. Nobody imagined anything like that would ever occur around here."

Emily said, "What *did* happen, exactly? I know a man collapsed in the front row of the magic show. Can you fill me in on what happened from that point?"

"Yes, well, I can tell you from my point of view as the emergency room nurse on duty that night. I don't know all the circumstances leading up to the incident."

"Tell me what you do know."

"I work as a nurse in the emergency ward of the Higginson Mills Hospital. The night the patient arrived by ambulance was particularly busy. We had already treated two victims for injuries sustained in accidents caused by the poor driving conditions during the rainstorm. As usual at this time of year, there were the standard flu cases. Parents get nervous at bedtime when their children cannot sleep due to coughing and fevers. Later on, some of the regulars came in; they get lonely and need someone to talk to. The hospital is always a place where they will get attention. There was at least a six-hour wait for non-urgent cases.

All the emergency rooms were full, and patients were on stretchers in the hallways.

"We got a call from the ambulance crew at the Emerald Hill gymnasium. An unidentified man had collapsed during a show, and he showed signs of severe respiratory failure and possible cardiac arrest. Seizures complicated the presentation of symptoms. They were unsure how to proceed. Usually in cases of heart attack or stroke, the paramedics perform initial first aid. In the ambulance, they have defibrillators and initial drug treatments to stabilize a cardiac condition, but the patient's conflicting signs confused their diagnosis. They consulted with the doctor on duty as to how to proceed. As he advised them on the radio, Dr. Guerison told us to set up video conferencing with specialists at the Ottawa General Hospital. We prepared the room specially equipped for heart and stroke cases. Due to the complicated signs exhibited by the patient, the first responders followed procedures for several possible outcomes.

"As it turned out, we could not save the victim's life. He died from asphyxiation shortly after arrival at the hospital. His whole body was in muscle contractions. He lapsed into a coma and passed away before the doctors could diagnose the cause of illness."

"Was there anything unusual about the case?" Emily asked. "Surely you must lose patients from time to time under similar circumstances."

Bonnie shook her head. "As the nurse assigned to his case, I had a very uneasy feeling about the whole affair. Too many factors didn't line up."

Emily also had already begun to suspect foul play. Several underlying impressions niggled at her investigative instinct. She reviewed the sequence of events at the magic show. First, there was the suspicious collapse of a dark stranger in the first row; then the man with the cowboy boots so rudely stepped on her foot while shoving his way towards the exit. He purposefully ignored Pete's attempt to return the glove and scarf. Then he sped away in a black Jeep, as if during a getaway.

Detectives should always pursue their hunches.

Emily urged Bonnie to continue. She needed to confirm more details to satisfy her gut feeling that this was no ordinary case of sudden death. "Can you tell me more about your suspicions?"

Bonnie was a capable and conscientious driver. She kept her eyes focussed on the road, yet her hands gripped the steering wheel with a steel grip, when she needed to stabilize her erratic nerves. Emily thought she detected a snatch of fear in the way Bonnie sucked in her breath before she began to speak again.

"For one thing, the patient had no identification papers on him. No driver's license, no credit cards, no nothing. Not even a toothpick in his pockets. Who goes out of his house without any money, without any ID? He was also totally alone that night. Why was he alone? No one in that whole auditorium, in such a small town, knew who he was? No one came with him to the hospital, and no one has reported him missing.

"Then, he had no signs of illness leading up to his collapse. He seemed to be a healthy male around 45 years old. He was sitting in the front row of a show, with the hall filled with hundreds of people. How could it be that nobody noticed any signs of distress? He simply fell down, dying with no warning. There were no signs of a struggle. What disease would kill a man so quickly without symptoms? More to the point, what weapon would kill a man so quickly with no signs of violence?"

"Bonnie, your observations are very accurate."

At that point, Bonnie allowed her gaze to stray from the road. Emily could see the whites of her eyes. The girl was obviously afraid, as if she had seen danger close enough to feel personally threatened.

"Oh, it gets a lot better than that. Just before he died, the patient was struggling for his last breath. Dr. Guerison came running into the room, desperately calling for help. He had been researching the case on the Internet. The doctor was looking for an extreme emergency response initiative kit. I didn't even know such a thing existed. We have a kit for Ebola virus. Apparently, the military have an auto-injector as an antidote for chemical weapons poisoning. In any case, it was too late. The patient died on the gurney.

"Only at that point did I notice he had a tattoo on his left shoulder. Jack Blossom, Canadian Platoon VX. I guess it was Roman numerals identifying his military assignment. I immediately recognized the name. My father used to talk about young Jack in the old days, when he coached the kids for the fiddling competitions."

"What exactly are you saying, Bonnie?" Emily asked, afraid of the answer.

Bonnie pulled the car over to the shoulder of the road. She could no longer concentrate on driving and talking at the same time. They were around the corner from Emily's house, but Emily refrained from giving directions.

"Jack Blossom died of chemical weapons poisoning." The response fell into a well of silence. Bonnie continued in a trembling voice. "We were all at risk, Detective Blossom! Every one of us who handled the patient could have been poisoned ourselves. Jack died almost immediately by inhaling a highly concentrated lethal dose of a deadly toxin."

By this time, tears flowed down Bonnie's cheeks. She held Emily's hands in hers in an iron grip of desperation. "They told us we were not in danger. None of us came in direct contact with the product. Thank goodness, we followed correct procedures and protocol."

In a gentle tone, Emily soothed Bonnie's nerves until the young nurse could get control over her fright. "You are a very brave woman, and you are a very good nurse. Every day, you risk your life to save other people in need. You did the right thing and followed procedures correctly. You could not save Jack's life, but you will save many others in the future. Put this experience aside, as difficult as it is, and move on."

Soon Bonnie got a hold of herself. She blew her nose, wiped her tears away and took control of the wheel.

"I'll get out here, my dear," Emily said with her hand on the door handle. "Thank you so much for the ride, and for the talk. Your story is safe with me. Don't worry. We'll get to the bottom of this." Then she added best wishes as if they were a lucky charm, "Safe home, my dear. Safe home."

Chapter 23

GARDEN OF PLENTY

My Star, shining brightly in the distant darkness,

You are at that stage now when you are always asking, Why?

There will be times in your life when you will not understand.

Why is the sky blue? Why can't you do as you please? Why do people smile when they are sad? Why do people cry when they are happy? Where does love come from? Why are people so mean to one another? Why can we not have what we want? Why is life so unfair?

Look around you, my darling. The answers surround you in the cycles of the universe. The plants and trees will be your teachers.

Daisy's garden is a jumble of love. Every spring, a simple plot of black, rich soil bursts forth. With the arrival of the warm sunshine and gentle rains, tiny green shoots emerge from their hiding places. They grow every day, just as you do. Each tiny plant will reveal the secret of who she is. Squash has fat leaves; carrots sprout into tiny, delicate lace; tomato leaves smell tangy; fennel tastes just like liquorice. Radishes are always eager to pop their heads up from the soil before the others, but corn is fickle, like dancers slow to raise their arms to the sun.

Daisy used to explain to me how every plant likes the friendship of her neighbours. Daisy's not good at controlling the chaos of joyful sprouting. Her vegetables grow where their seeds have fallen. She tries to make some sense of it all, but the plants have their own will. She is not good at weeding out the useless, inedible, unattractive ones.

Still, there are always plenty of purple runner beans; heady, bright sunflowers; luscious, plump zucchini; and rainbow chard.

Everyone feasts on the garden. The chickens scratch for worms. The peacocks peck the bugs. Friday likes to make his bed in the cool shade of the towering giants. Daisy searches through the weeds for vegetables for dinner.

"Never mind," says Daisy, "There's plenty of food for us all."

As the summer progresses, the jumble of joy becomes a jungle of taste, colour and smell. All the plants vie for their space. Some blossom. Some wilt and die, leaving room for others to flourish. Health is beauty.

The fragile disappear. The strong thrive.

This is the way of the earth.

Chapter 24

STAR-CROSSED CASSIOPEIA

By the time Emily arrived home, the clock was chiming twelve. Charlie was waiting by the door, as she expected he would. He looked dishevelled and annoyed.

"Cinderella made it home just in time," Emily said. "You should be happy to see me, my handsome Prince Charming."

The cat seemed far from pleased. His snub nose pointed to the ceiling, his ears were flat back and his fur on the top of his head stood on end. He rolled his slanted eyes, as if he had been deserted and abandoned for days. Even his fluffy coat appeared matted. His tail was listless, dragging along the carpet. As he accompanied her, he practically staggered to the kitchen.

However, as soon as she reached for his favourite cat treats, he miraculously regained his energetic happiness.

"You are a man without principles," Emily said. "Lovers-for-hire have short memories. You are an unscrupulous wretch. You treat your dear, generous owner as if I were a dish mop." She paused, reconsidering her statement. "On second thought, you are the mop, and I am the rag. If I were not so upset, I'd go directly to bed, but after all we've been through, I think we deserve a cup of tea, something soothing."

She rustled through the cupboard full of boxes of assorted tea.

"Liquorice with a touch of lavender. That should do the trick," she murmured. "And you, my Mr. Man, shall have a teaspoon full of tuna, just to make us both feel better after your long, trying day of sleeping."

She bustled around the kitchen, prepared the tea and then settled into her armchair in the living room. She placed her slippered feet on the petit-point footstool and drew a cozy afghan around her legs. The cat quickly deposited himself in her lap.

The clock ticked. The cat purred. The teaspoon rattled in the sugar bowl. Her teacup clinked into its saucer into its porcelain security. Sounds of comfort and safety surrounded the weary detective. Soon the gentle sounds of snoring completed her aura of slumber in the depth of night.

She woke with a start when the clock donged the hour at three in the morning. The cat stretched and planted his claws into her thigh. When she moved, her muscles were sore and stiff. At first, she forgot where she was and could not remember the uneasy revelations that had disturbed her sleep. Then she reached for the telephone. She dialled a number automatically, as if she had continued from dreaming to waking in one instant of realization. She listened intently as the ring tone repeated at the other end of the line.

"Three, four, five … Will he never pick up?"

Finally, an impatient voice answered groggily. "What the hell's the matter now?"

"Are you sleeping?" she said in a small voice that was almost a whisper.

"I was. What the hell do you expect? What f-ing time is it, anyway?"

"Pete, are you feeling all right?"

"Feeling all right? No. I'm bloody sleeping—at least, I was. Why are you calling at this time of the night?"

"Morning." She felt obliged to correct him just so he knew she knew what time it was. "It's three in the morning. Can you come over?"

"Come over? Now? It's three in the morning! Hell, no! Why should I do that?"

"I just want to be sure you're okay."

"I'm okay."

I want you to tell me that you're fine."

"I'm fine."

"Are you feeling well?"

"I'm feeling well. Now, go to bed and go to sleep and don't call again."

"I don't have to worry?"

"Emily, what are you babbling about? I'm fine. I'm sleeping. And I don't intend to get up yet. There's no auction to go to, no sale, no flea market. Now, I'm going back to sleep. You go back to sleep. We'll meet in the morning. Then you'll tell me what this is all about."

"Where will you be?"

"I'll meet you at Missy's at seven. She's the only place open for coffee that early."

"Missy's at seven. I'll be there."

When Emily uncurled herself from her favourite armchair on her way to bed, she noticed a snippet of paper poking out from underneath the cushion. Without thinking, she pulled the letter from its hiding place. The handwriting was familiar. It was a letter addressed to Corporal Jack Blossom. The return address was from Carly MacLeod.

"This must have been included in the batch of letters I rescued from Jack's house," she mused, absentmindedly extracting the letter from the envelope. The single page was tattered and torn at the edges, as if it had been read and handled over and over. The paper was stained, and the ink was smudged, as if from tears. Emily recognized the handwriting, with flared swirls and delicate punctuation.

Dear Jack,

By the time you receive this letter, you will know the truth about me. The voices have shown me the way. They are right, of course. I am not worthy of living.

Now, you must come home to look after your daughter. Aster needs you more than I do. Unlike me, she deserves your love. I promise you that you really are her father. Surely you remember that wonderful night when she was conceived under the full moon.

Life has never been more beautiful. You always were my dearest one. I'm sorry I never measured up.

Goodbye is such a difficult word to say. I have always loved you.

Until forever,

Carly

Emily carefully folded the letter and slipped the worn page into the envelope. She deposited it in the drawer beside the others wrapped in red ribbon.

Her steps were heavy as she pulled herself up the stairs by the banister. Never had she felt so old, so helpless. The cat's claws clicked on the carpet as he bounced ahead of her towards his cozy bed. She did not even respond to his plaintiff meow when she pulled the duvet over her head. Sleep was her only remedy for hopelessness.

Chapter 25

EARTH SHINE

In the deepest woods, the cycles are eternal. Towering, strong trees spread their branches high above the rich, dark earth, forming a canopy—a roof above the house of the forest. Roots intertwine with each other, making each single tree stronger in the embrace of her friend next door. Apple branch fingers interweave so that each clump of apple trees bears different-tasting fruits. Maples and elms spread wide, leafy skirts around their feet. The sun nourishes their puffy buds, shiny leaves and helicopter seeds.

Some trees are not strong. They cannot compete for the sun puddles in the depths of the dark woods. They weaken and grow spindly. Their leaves wither and die. They step aside and shed their bark; branches eventually break. They fall to the earth and become nourishment for the stronger trees of the forest.

Amongst the plants and trees, there is no right or wrong. Life cycles. Seeds sprout. Roots spread. Leaves burst from bud to blossom, then dry and fall as autumn soils freeze to winter crystals. There is no such thing as death. All life continues in forms we may not recognize. Spring brings forth nourishment for beginnings in new birth.

When you wonder why, my darling, look to the earth and her friends for the answers. Your name is Aster Blossom after a beautiful flower. You will understand. We are part of it all.

Chapter 26

FIRST STAR

Aster lay on her bed, tucked underneath the sloping ceiling. Her head was propped on her hands so that she could look out the tiny window under the eaves. As the blue sky darkened to night, she waited for the first star to appear just above the pale horizon. As soon as she discerned a faint twinkling, she repeated a familiar rhyme aloud.

> Star light, star bright,
> First star I see tonight,
> I wish I may, I wish I might
> Have the wish I wish tonight.

Then she closed her eyes tight shut, pinched up her cheeks, and repeated the wish she had made every night since she could remember. *I wish I could have my very own kitten.*

The next morning she woke, bright and early, as soon as the sun peeked through the lace curtains. She dressed and tiptoed down the stairs so she wouldn't wake Daisy. After pulling on her barn coat, she let herself outside, closely accompanied by Friday, who was not about to let her out of his sight. The animals were still sleeping when she entered the stable.

By now, she was familiar with the farm routine. She loved going by herself into the barn, listening to the animals munching on their feed and conversing with each of the beasts in turn. She came to know them as her friends. She no longer felt as lonely as she had been in the tiny log house where she'd grown up.

As an only child, she was used to fending for herself, but she was often lonely. She imagined that a kitten would be the very best companion: Someone whom she could talk to, tell her secrets to; someone who would understand her and be her very special pal. However, she could never convince either of her parents to let her have a pet.

Her mother, Carly, said she could not cope with having any more to look after than a child and a house. It was all she could do to keep up with the housework, dishes and cooking. Besides, she said that cats terrified her.

After Jack came home, he absolutely forbade Aster from even mentioning the idea of having a cat in the house. "I love you dearly," he always said. "But don't ask again. The subject is off limits."

In some ways, Aster was accustomed to having what she wanted. Both her parents were happy to oblige her tastes in food and dress; satisfying her desires spared them the necessity of making their own decisions. They also avoided arguments by giving in to their only child's wants and whims.

However, having a kitten was never negotiable. The answer was always no.

Since Aster could remember, her mother had always been a sad person in need of reassurance and affection. Her essence was insatiable desire. Nothing her daughter could do or say would make her happy. Aster was all too familiar with the smile that trembled at the edges of her mother's lips, as if tragedy might strike away any glimmer of hope at any second.

With childlike optimism, the toddler had learned to find her own inner happiness within the realm of her imagination. As she grew, her games and imaginary playmates provided simple joys, bringing her pleasure in spite of her mother's constant negativity. When she learned to read, she escaped into the pages of fantasy and fairy tales.

Her mother timed her own death to coincide with the day that Jack returned from overseas. Aster was too young to know the symptoms of desperate depression. When she saw her mother empty the contents of a bottle full of pills into her mouth, she could not have known the fatal consequences that would follow.

The night of Jack's scheduled arrival, the child was beside herself with excitement. Finally, she would get to know her own father, the man who had written her mysteriously wondrous letters, the soldier who had been fighting a war and defending Canada on the other side of the world. She conjectured that his return would bring happiness to her grey world, coexisting with a shadow mother who seemed utterly incapable of unfettered joy.

Upon her father's return, ecstasy was short-lived. After the funeral, father and daughter settled into another kind of gloom. Soon the youngster learned to be the mother herself, looking after and cooking and cleaning for a man who rarely smiled, whose eyes wore blank stares and dark glances. By rereading his letters from the desert, she tried to remember the father she had imagined. She revisited her dreams of the man she was convinced he would be in real life. Desperately she tried to erase her disappointment when he failed to answer her questions, ignored her presence or—even worse—seemed to take her for granted.

When the time came, she was well prepared to escape the drab shanty home. Her father repeated the procedure over and again, like a soldier training his troops for disaster. Together they stuffed her backpack with basic clothing, toothbrush and teddy bear. He made her repeat back to him the code and signals she would recognize when the time came for her to make her escape. He drove her to Daisy's farm gate and rehearsed which way she would ride her bicycle to safety by the back roads.

She learned the scenario the way a soccer player would learn drills and tactics for winning. Her father was her coach. She wanted to please him, to be his champion, number one player. She poured all her child's love for her father into being the best little champion on the planet. He rewarded her with a smile and a pat on the back. When she knew the routine backwards and forwards, finally his worry seemed to alleviate into a faint relaxation of the shoulders, a twinkle in his eye. All was ready for her to step into her future.

Strangely, she never questioned the purpose of their plan. She accepted the tactics at face value. She would do as he trained her to do, without asking why.

When Aster Blossom arrived on Daisy's doorstep, the loneliness of isolated childhood melted into the embrace of a giant, warm and cuddly dog. Daisy's world was populated with loving creatures and unquestioned acceptance. She felt as if she had finally found a home.

Only one small detail was still missing, until the morning when Pete's pickin' truck pulled in the driveway. Friday announced the arrival of a stranger with a low, urgent bark. Aster took out running from the barn, leaping like a rabbit across the barnyard, to notify Daisy of the visitor's arrival.

Farmer Blossom was just emerging from the house, manipulating her bulky chore coat over her shoulders as she lumbered across the driveway. When Daisy recognized whose truck was sitting in the driveway, she hurriedly brushed the straggling hair from her face and tried to smooth her clothes down over her awkward bulges. Aster noticed Daisy's cheeks flushed. The bashful woman seemed oddly nervous in a giggly sort of way.

Pete rolled down the window when Daisy approached the truck. The child watched from the distance of her perch in the doorway of the barn, with her hand stroking Friday's huge head. She could see the two of them chatting, softly throwing sentences back and forth, and occasionally glancing in Aster's direction. Laughter punctuated their banter. They both seemed quite pleased to be in each other's company. Eventually they reached some sort of conclusion to their discussion. Then they simultaneously beckoned in her direction.

"Aster—Star, honey," Daisy called out with a lilt in her voice. "Mr. Picken has brought you a present."

Slowly Aster left the safety of her vantage point. She was afraid to appear too eager. She had lived her entire, short life learning to accept disappointment, almost as surely as she hoped for unmitigated joy. She did not yet trust the pleasure of her new surroundings.

She could hardly believe her ears when she heard Daisy say, "Pete has brought you a kitten."

Sure enough, when Aster approached the truck, Daisy put her hand on the child's shoulder and pointed into the cab. On Pete's lap was a tiny grey kitten with eyes of gold brightly shining up at Aster.

Unbelieving, she gasped, looking first at Daisy's broad grin and then at Pete's smile from underneath his moustache. "Really? A kitten for me?"

When she reached for the kitten, she could hear purring almost before she could feel its tiny body innocently allowing itself to cuddle into her embrace.

Aster Blossom knew immediately that she had finally found a true friend.

Chapter 27

SHABBY CHIC

Pete Picken was a practical man. He lived in the moment and was constantly on the go, pursuing many interests.

To earn his living, he was an antique dealer. He spent a considerable part of his days driving around the countryside in his truck, scavenging. Picking is a term of the trade that refers to the art of hunting for antiques at the source. The sign on his pickup read "Picken and His Truck."

"You're only as good as the last deal you made," he would say to anyone who would listen.

To spend his hard-earned money, Pete was a farmer. That is to say, he made hay with antique machinery, using tractors that seldom ran without breaking.

Throughout the year, he organized community events in Emerald Hill. Pete made it his business to know what was going on in town. He appointed himself Emerald Hill's one-man, better-village advocate.

When the annual fair came to town, local farmers and townspeople volunteered to put the event together. Twenty committees orchestrated competitions that included the calf show for the 4Hers, dairy and beef competitions, three horse shows for light saddle horses and pulling teams and driving hitches for heavy horses including Percherons and Clydesdales. Pete helped to stage many of the activities involved with the busiest weekend of the year. His duties included serving at the beer tent staging the bands, announcing the parade and controlling the safety of the demolition derbies for cars and combines. There was an infinite variety of duties involved with hosting thousands of visitors to a small town of 1,200.

As summer approached, Mr. Picken had a lot on his mind. All of his energy focussed on the tasks he set for himself each day. He did not put time aside for the unnecessary.

Emily Blossom was a challenge in Pete's life. On the one hand, he appreciated her energy and enthusiasm. She actually believed she could change the world. He admired her optimism, even if he considered her hopelessly idealistic. On the other hand, she never ceased to disrupt his intentional myopia. She was a hard person to ignore, especially when she called him at 3:00 a.m.

Suffice it to say that Pete Picken was not in the best of moods when he drove along Main Street in the early morning. He felt conflicted when he spotted Emily waiting on the doorstep of Missy's Place. She disturbed his self-absorption.

"Your sweater's buttoned up crooked," he said even before he got out of the truck. "You're wearing socks of a different colour. That's not like you. What the hell's the matter now?"

"Can't you even say good morning before you start in on being a grouch?"

Pete was surprised to catch Detective Blossom off guard. Emily usually looked neat and tidy, except for a stray lock of hair that persisted in falling over her left eye. She fumbled at the buttons with trembling hands.

He brusquely pushed past her reaching for the door.

"Wait, Pete," she practically pleaded with him. "I need to ask you …" She paused, searching for words. Her gaze wandered and eventually settled on his face. She peered into his eyes with a worried squint. "Are you sure you're feeling all right?"

"Emily, cut that out!" he said. Her staring at him made him very uncomfortable. He did not like being interrogated. "I'm fine. I just need a good strong cup of coffee." He reached for the door again.

"No really. You're not feeling faint, lightheaded, twitchy? As if you're going to pass out?"

"Emily, I've about had enough. Tell me what this is all about."

Emily looked away uncertainly. Without an explanation, she switched topics. "You did say you picked up a glove and a scarf at the magic show the other night, didn't you? You did say you picked them up and put them in your truck?"

"Yes, I did say that. Actually, I put them in that milk can in the back of the truck. I lifted the lid and threw them inside so they wouldn't get wet. I'll show you."

He reached for the lid of the can, but she leapt at him, grabbing his arm away with very uncharacteristic panic. "No, no, don't do that!" she cried. "Don't touch it! Leave it be!"

At this point, the usually calm and cool detective was frantically pulling at his sleeve, tugging him away from the truck.

"Emily, cut that out!" Pete put his large farmer's hands on her arms, pinning her feet to the ground. He stared into the depths of her eyes as she tried to look away. Tears brimmed on the rims of her eyelids.

He surprised them both when he took her in his strong arms and hugged her tightly. He could feel her trembling as he held her, willing her to calm her shaken nerves. She spoke into his coat. He could barely make out the muffled words.

"I'm so afraid you're going to die," she said. "You touched the murder weapon. It's deadly poison. You could drop dead at any minute, like Jack Blossom did. I don't know what I'd do without you."

He held her until her sobbing quieted. Then he positioned her frail body so that he could look at her straight on. His face was so close to hers that he could feel her breath on his lips. "Emily, look at me." He paused and then continued in a soft whisper. "Nothing's going to happen to me. I'm not going to die. I'm fine. Get a hold of yourself."

She sniffled like a child, looked away and began to rummage in her purse. He handed her a napkin from his pocket. She blew her nose loudly, wiped her cheeks and took a deep sigh. "I need a coffee too," she said in a little girl's voice. "I'm so sorry, Pete. I'll tell you everything. There's so much sadness in the world."

He reached for the door and held her arm as she stepped into the shop. Never before had he realized how fragile she was, disguised in fashionable clothes.

Chapter 28

CIRCUMSTANTIAL EVIDENCE

With only three tables for customers, Missy's Place was even quainter than the Country Kitchen on the Hill. Missy fed both her family and the townsfolk in the kitchen of her own home. The menu was the same every day: rich chocolate brownies, sugary lemon squares, Montreal bagels and homemade soup: From early morning until late afternoon, clients served themselves hot soup, fresh buns and strong coffee. All day long, Missy prepared casseroles, hot buttered chicken and shepherd's pie. She sold take-home meals, ready to eat for busy working households where no one had time to do their own cooking.

Her cupboards were full with local produce, honey, garlic, jams and jellies. Missy had a weakness for buying knick-knacks at auction; she offered them for sale as hostess gifts. Most of her clients were in a hurry to get errands done so they could be at home with the kids after a long day at work. She offered one-stop shopping.

Missy was one of those good Christians who saved wayward souls in spite of herself. She was in a constant struggle with her conscience. She needed to make money with a small shop in a town where residents preferred to take their business elsewhere. She ended up providing hospitality for folks who had nowhere to go and no one to talk to. They shared their life stories as Missy bustled around the kitchen. After hours of chatter, they paid the cost of a coffee and left with free lemon squares or burnt buns that Missy claimed were not good enough for her regular clients. Missy could easily carry on a running commentary on Who's Who in Emerald Hill, however she liked to think that she was selective about whom she told what to. She did not like to spread gossip unless she deemed it absolutely necessary to correct rampant misinformation from flying about town.

When Pete and Emily entered, Missy turned her back. She pretended she had not witnessed their animated conversation outside on her door stoop. She picked up a bowl and began furiously beating at batter that she had already thoroughly whipped. From over her shoulder, she greeted them with a cheerful, "Good morning! I'll be with you shortly. I've just got to put these muffins in the oven. Make yourselves at home, as usual. Help yourselves to the coffee. It's freshly made and piping hot."

Missy went about her baking as quietly as possible. She did not want to miss a word of their conversation. At first, Pete and Emily tried to whisper, but as they became less aware of her presence, she could overhear most of the discussion.

Emily began by telling Pete that she had hitchhiked to McInness Hall.

"Are you crazy?" Pete was not good at keeping his voice down.

"I wanted to know more about the young Jack Blossom. I knew he played the fiddle. I needed to track down someone who knew him as a teenager. I knew I would find that person at the Strawberry Social." When Pete opened his mouth to comment, she quickly interjected, "Don't interrupt. I'll tell you everything."

"What has this got to do with the milk can?"

"I'm getting to that in a minute. You have to be patient."

Missy could tell that Pete was not exactly good at exercising patience. However, she also realized that she was hardly the most discreet eavesdropper. Nevertheless, they both managed to listen while Emily recounted her experience at McInness. She repeated Angus's story of the fight between Jack Blossom and Frankie Duval over Carly McLeod.

"I still don't know what this has to do with the milk can," Pete repeated, drumming his fingers on the table.

Emily patted the back of his hands. "I haven't gotten to that part yet," she said "That comes when I got the ride home with ..."

"Don't tell me you hitchhiked back to the Hill!"

"No, no. I got a ride from a nice girl who gave me a lift."

"You *did* hitchhike! Have you got no sense at all?"

"Listen to me, Pete. I'm getting to the part about the murder weapon."

"Get on with it, then."

"I can't stand the suspense," said Missy, who gave up all efforts to restrain herself. With the muffins safely stowed in the oven, she approached their table, wiping her hands on her apron. "Are we talking about Jack Blossom, who comes in here all the time? His daughter, Aster, loves my shepherd's pie. Come to think of it, I haven't seen him recently. I was wondering where he was."

Pete looked at Emily as if to say, "Who invited her?" However, Emily seemed oblivious to the interruption of her narrative, so Missy sat down to join them.

"Bonnie MacDonell was the nurse on duty at the emergency room when they brought Jack in to the hospital after he collapsed at the magic show."

"Jack's dead?" Missy could not believe her ears.

"They said it was a heart attack or a stroke. How do you know he was murdered?" Pete asked.

Missy interrupted again. "I didn't see Jack's death in the obituaries. I love to read the obituaries. You learn so much about people. You have to admire the way some people lived their lives. So-and-so ran his business for 50 years, volunteered for several charity organizations. He left behind his loving wife, three lovely children and two grandchildren. Everyone leads such perfect lives according to the obituaries."

Pete repeated his question to Emily. "How do you know Jack was murdered?"

Missy continued as if she had not heard. "I wonder what they'll say about me when I'm gone?"

Emily said to Pete, "I'm getting to that part."

Missy motored on. "You have to read the obits to know what goes on around town. It's sad to say, but everybody is dying these days. You never know who will be next."

"Bonnie described his gruesome death," said Emily, finally getting to the point of the whole story. "They isolated him before he died. The doctor suspected chemical weapons poisoning. He died before they could confirm the exact cause of death."

Pete slammed his hand on the table so hard that the cups bounced. "That's just like you! You get half the story and then jump to conclusions. I knew it!"

Emily remained calm with wide, innocent eyes. Half a smile tickled the edge of her lips. "Bonnie told me that anyone coming in contact with such extremely potent toxins could die within minutes."

Missy eagerly dove into an explanation. "I've heard about those weapons of mass destruction on TV. The Syrians used them in the Middle East. Saddam Hussein used them against the Kurds."

A quizzical expression crossed Pete's face. "I cannot conceive of a weapon of mass destruction," he said.

"Such weapons are highly illegal. How would anyone get hold of something like that?" said Missy. "Why would anyone use that stuff at all, especially here in Canada?"

"Maybe to kill a soldier who served in the Canadian army in the Middle East," said Emily softly. "Maybe there's some kind of a link to Jack's military past when he was stationed there."

"A couple of weeks ago, Jack *was* here with a stranger," Missy interjected. "A man from the mountains. Jack and this chap were in the army together. They spoke for a long time. I couldn't hear the conversation, but I know they had an argument. I overheard Jack say, 'You leave my daughter out of this!' Jack was very upset. He forgot his shepherd's pie. Come to think of it, that's the last time I saw him."

"So this is where the milk can comes in," said Pete.

"Precisely," Emily said, squeezing his hand with her tiny fingers.

"What milk can?" Missy glanced from one face to another, trying to decipher the unspoken messages travelling between them.

"The murder weapon could be in Pete's truck."

Pete gasped, finally making the connection between Emily's revelations and his own well-being—or lack thereof.

"So what if it is?"

"Inspector Allard needs to know about it."

"No way. They'll confiscate my truck."

"How will we get it into the hands of the police to confirm whether or not the scarf was actually used as a murder weapon?"

"We'll put it on the sidewalk, call the station and tell them to come pick it up."

"They'll trace the phone call," said Missy with a tremor. "Please don't leave it outside my shop. That would be the end of my business."

"I'll drive it to the police station in the middle of the night and leave it outside the front door."

"Someone might open it by mistake. They'd be killed immediately from the fumes."

"I'll leave a note."

Emily clicked her tongue against the roof of her mouth, as if she were scolding a small boy. Missy cringed at her audacity.

"Pete, for the sake of humanity …"

"What!" he exclaimed, holding his palms out with a shrug of the shoulders in exaggerated innocence. "What's humanity got to do with it?" He paused and then continued. "Why do I care about humanity, anyway?"

Missy looked at one and then the other. Emily kindly waited for him to come to his own inevitable conclusion. He stared back and forth between them, searching for some sign of pity or empathy.

"Yeah, right! I'm going to drive right on down to the police station and tell Inspector Allard I just happen to have a weapon of mass destruction used to kill poor old Jack Blossom. The murder weapon just happens to be in a milk can in the back of my truck! You ladies are dreaming in Technicolor."

They simply stared back at him without comment.

"I'm gonna take it to the dump. That's where it belongs."

"What happens if someone sees a perfectly good milk can over there and takes it home? You'd never forgive yourself, Pete."

"Wanna bet?"

Missy shouldered the heaviness of the silence in the room. Pete took a deep breath of resignation and looked at Emily sideways. "They'll have to pay me twenty-five bucks for the milk can."

Still, Emily said nothing.

"I paid twenty dollars for the thing."

She blinked. He blinked. Missy blinked.

"Well, I have to make at least enough to pay for my gas."

Finally, Emily ended the stalemate.

"I'll go with you," she said. "I'll talk to Allard and put in a good word for you. I'll explain everything. He'll understand."

Pete stood up and headed for the door.

"You pay for the coffee. I'll be waiting in the truck."

Emily reached for her purse and put five dollars on the counter. "Where did that man live in the mountains?" Emily asked Missy.

"What man?"

"The one who was with Jack Blossom two weeks ago."

"He said he lived in the bush."

"What bush?"

"Somewhere up in the hills, across the river in Quebec. He said he lived in the bush, on land belonging to the monastery. The monks let him live in the forest. The whole conversation seemed very strange. Jack looked as if he had seen a ghost. Do you think …?"

Pete honked the horn, and Emily rushed after him without responding to Missy's unfinished question.

The smell of burning muffins pervaded Missy's kitchen. She hurried to extract them from the oven. Maybe a few were salvageable for her regular customers. She would give the remainder of the scorched ones to the hangers-on.

Chapter 29

PROFESSIONAL PRIVILEGE

Emily thought of the police station as her office, her home base when she needed professional status. She considered Inspector Allard her mentor. She had great respect for his expertise and tactful discipline.

A detective must cultivate her garden of resources. The police can be useful to an undercover sleuth who prefers to remain inconspicuous. Uniformed defenders of the law have access to information unavailable to the public. Working in collaboration with the regulatory forces can often advance a covert investigation, thus bringing the culprit to justice more quickly. Cooperation is often the best means to access classified information. As well, in some cases, the sleuth herself can be of considerable benefit to police officers.

The sprawling building was practical and understated. Nothing about the architecture of the police station in Hamilton Mills suggested imposing authority. The squat brick facade boasted few windows and only one heavy door to the lobby. Visitors did not exactly feel welcome to drop in for a friendly chat. The offices were functional and discreet.

Detective Emily Blossom assumed a certain privilege when entering the police headquarters. As a detective of some renown, Mrs. Blossom considered that this edifice was where she belonged. She had to tug hard to heave the door open, but once in the lobby, she adopted a distinct air of ownership.

However, she was very surprised by her reception.

"Inspector Allard is unavailable," said the clerk.

"How can that be?" said Emily. "I know he is usually in at this time of the morning, reviewing his cases. At precisely eight o'clock, he prepares his constables for the day's strategy."

"You are not included in the present investigation. I have been given specific instructions not to allow you access to the premises." The receptionist peered over her glasses through the bulletproof window between her office and the foyer where Emily stood. Her attitude implied an air of superiority over the common rabble who did not know better than to recognize her elevated status. Her haughty demeanour dared anyone to assume that she was a mere peon among ordinary folk.

In one way, Emily was flattered. Being singled out as an unwelcome intruder was a form if appreciation. Inspector Allard must have recognized her clever prowess. No doubt, by now he realized she was on the same trail of inquiry as he was. That he did not want her assistance concerning the murder of Jack Blossom meant he considered her a significant rival to his acumen.

Now she simply had to convince him that she could be of assistance, rather than a hazard.

In addition, there was Pete Picken to consider. He was still waiting in the parking lot in his beloved truck, with the murder weapon stowed safely away in a milk can among his antiques. Luckily, Pete was enjoying a pipe full of fresh tobacco she had purchased for him on their way to the station. He would be happily distracted as long as his pipe remained lit. Time was of the essence.

This meant that she had to speak to Inspector Allard in person as soon as possible.

Undaunted by a mere receptionist, Emily considered her options. Surely there was a back entrance to the police headquarters. She had never seen any constables entering through the front lobby.

She thanked the snooty clerk in spite of her poor assistance. *Even in the face of temptation and justification, a detective must never burn her bridges.*

The lithe and stealthy sleuth slipped outside. A wisp of smoke wafted from the slit of Pete's side window, indicating he was still contentedly puffing away. Before he spotted her in his rear-view mirror, she scurried around the corner to the back of the building.

As a person of tiny stature, Emily could hide in very small places. She tucked herself behind a cruiser parked near the rear entrance. Soon her patience paid off. An officer arrived, slammed his car door and strode quickly towards the building. Emily guessed he was late for the early morning briefing.

He threw the door open and rushed inside. Emily was as close behind him as his shadow.

She almost had time to breathe a sigh of relief and congratulate herself for her cleverness when alarm bells sounded a shrill alert. Before she could reconnoitre, five very large police officers surrounded her, pointing guns straight at her head. The muzzle of one rifle was so close to her nose that she could see into the mouth of the barrel. It trembled in the hands of the constable holding his weapon. She wordlessly dropped her purse with a thud and raised her hands above her head.

Inspector Albert Allard came running to see what the ruckus was about.

Emily gushed with joy. "Allo, Allard. There you are, my friend! Comment ça va? That silly person at the front desk told me you weren't in yet. I knew you'd be here bright and early. We detectives don't have time to sleep in, do we?"

She dropped her arms to her side and approached the astonished inspector, who was quite obviously caught off guard. Emily clutched at his sleeve and gathered him into her confidence. Standing on tiptoes, she whispered towards his ear, "I need to speak with you in person."

She glanced around at her captors, who lowered their rifles in embarrassment. Then with the towering inspector in tow, she headed for his office. Having been there several times in her recent career as an astute detective, she knew its location well.

"Mrs. Blossom, you could have been severely injured out there. Have you no sense of caution?"

"My dear, at my age, I have no time to waste. Besides, I know your men are reasonable. They are employed to put fear into the hearts of men. Need I remind you? I do not fall into that category."

With little ceremony, Emily escorted Allard to his swivel chair and pulled up a chair opposite to the desk. While sitting straight and proper on the edge of her seat, she clutched her purse in her lap. "Now, I shall get right to the point. I know you're a busy man."

However, she paused before proceeding. She pulled off her gloves one finger at a time, folded them precisely together and unsnapped the clasp on her purse to insert them inside. The closing purse clicked with finality, like a punctuation mark to something she had not yet said. Then she leaned towards the inspector with intently piercing eyes.

A detective should always use silence to build suspense. Keep him waiting. This tactic often tweaks the agent's curiosity. He will be more likely to cooperate.

"Inspector Allard, have we reached the point where we can call each other by our first names? May I call you Albert?"

"Mrs. Blossom, why exactly are you here?"

Emily opened her purse again and rummaged around for a handkerchief, stalling to consider how best to begin their discussion. "Inspector Allard, how far have you progressed in your investigation into the murder of Jack Blossom?"

Allard sputtered and stuttered. Emily surmised he hardly knew where to begin. She had him in the palm of her hand. She asked, "Have you determined the cause of death?"

Allard stood up and put his hand on the doorknob. "This interview is over," he said in a manner that suggested he had bitten into an unripe banana. "We have nothing to discuss on this matter."

Emily did not acknowledge his gesture of dismissal. She addressed his empty chair. Perhaps she had underestimated his underestimation of her detective skills, but she knew he would soon recapitulate. She continued calmly. "I believe that you have probably discovered that Corporal Blossom was murdered by a very lethal weapon never before used in this wonderful, peaceful country of Canada."

Allard remained standing, staring at her back.

She added, "The level of toxicity is indeed more dangerous than any known product of poison ever developed."

Allard returned and quietly sat back in his chair. She noticed his fingers gripped the armrests with white knuckles. His nostrils flared ever so slightly.

At this point, Emily decided to go out on a limb. "Such a product might even be used as a weapon of mass destruction. In the hands of the wrong people, hundreds, even thousands of innocent victims could be killed."

She paused again. Now she ventured slightly beyond her specific knowledge, into the realm of supposition. "In fact, this product may have already been used in foreign countries where the rules of war are slightly less regulated than we are over here in the so-called civilized world. The public outcry would be loud and swift if this news were ever to reach the media. Panic could ensue. Political heads would roll."

Until this point, Emily had kept her voice totally monotone. Then she assumed a childlike lilt.

"How could such a murder like this happen in a small town like Emerald Hill? Such an incident would certainly put us on the map, wouldn't it?"

She stopped speaking and waited for the stunned officer to compose himself.

He finally asked, "How do you know all this?"

She smiled ever so slightly. "I have my sources."

"Even my constables have been kept in the dark about this. Only the CIA knows about the gravity of the situation. I have been sworn to secrecy."

Now she could play her ace of spades without revealing her whole hand. "But you don't have the murder weapon, do you? Without proof, you are only going on supposition. You have no proof and no suspect. Isn't that correct?"

"Mrs. Blossom, are you withholding?"

She corrected him.

"*Detective* Blossom."

"Detective, need I remind you what the penalties are for withholding evidence?"

"I am here to cooperate to the fullest, my dear Inspector Allard. May I remind you that it is I who came here this morning, is it not? You are the one who tried to block me from seeing you."

"What have you got? What are you hiding?"

She ticked her tongue against the roof of her mouth, shaking her head in admonishment. "Dear, dear Allard, why do you think I would hide anything from you? What's in it for me to avoid sharing information with you? I'm not an enemy."

"No, but you've got something up your sleeve," he said. "I know you better than you think I do. I can tell by your snippy attitude. You think you're oh so clever."

She tittered. "Do I detect a little professional jealously, now, Inspector?"

He was becoming annoyed. Perhaps she was rubbing it in a little too far.

"I will tell you what I know, and what I suspect," she said. "But I have a few conditions to which you must agree."

"You're not in a great bargaining position, my dear lady," said Allard huffily. "May I remind you that you are speaking to an officer of the law? You do not have the right to refuse to give evidence."

Detective Emily Blossom gathered up her purse and her coat and stepped towards the door. Before she could turn the knob, the inspector blocked her way. He stared down at her in his most imposing manner. "Well, then?"

She returned to her seat. "I will tell you where the murder weapon is."

"Now we're getting somewhere." Allard sat down, clasping his hands together on the desk.

"But first you must agree to take possession of the container in which the weapon is stored without questioning how it got there. You must take the necessary safety precautions to make sure no one opens the container. No one shall examine its contents until they can be handled with the utmost care and security."

"Of course. Safety and security is essential. Is there anything else?"

"You may interrogate the person who found the evidence, but you may not arrest him or lay charges against him for any reason."

"Anything else?"

"It will cost you twenty-five dollars."

"Oh, come on! You're putting me on!" said Allard, losing his patience.

Emily relaxed and laughed, willing her eyes to twinkle. "I know it sounds ridiculous, but those are the conditions under which my source has agreed to cooperate with you. You must agree, or he will walk. Then, we will all be in danger."

The inspector stood up and reached out his hand across the desk. "You have a deal."

"Fine, then," Emily said, gathering up her coat again. "Follow me."

After working out the details of how best to extract the milk can from Pete's truck, and after Pete provided a description of the suspect, Emily and Pete were free to leave the station.

"Maybe you could use your hard-earned profits to buy me a cup of tea," said Emily on their way back to Emerald Hill. "At the least, I deserve a reward of some kind for getting you out of such a mess."

Without looking in the rear-view mirror, Pete slammed on the brakes in the middle of the highway and skidded to a stop. "Look who got who into a mess? It was all your idea to go to the magic show in the first place! I was happily minding my own business before you came along. You pay for your own tea."

She laughed and agreed easily. "I'm getting off cheap. At least I don't have to pay for yours too."

Chapter 30

ORION'S NEBULA

On a day like this, Daisy was tempted to bask in the warming sunshine. She sat on a patch of tender grass beside the riding ring and waited for Aster, who was preparing the pony for their first riding lesson. She leaned against a spruce tree with the cat purring in her lap and a sleepy Friday stretched out in a sun puddle beside her.

The scent of evergreen mingled with wafts of moist earth and sweet blossoms. Sounds of spring echoed across the fields beyond the barnyard. Birds twittered and chorused in the treetops, heralding their presence to all within range. One cardinal sang from the top of an ancient maple. "Here. Here. Here."

Another answered from the deep forest beyond the pasture. "Pretty girl, pretty, pretty, pretty."

Chickadees peeped; woodpeckers hammered; crows cawed and clucked; red-winged blackbirds chirruped. Canada Geese heralded their return, threading arrows across the lazy cloud sky.

Creatures returning from the south energized the rest of the world awakening from winter's hibernation. Splashing and gurgling, the stream through the gully overflowed its banks, tumbling and bubbling towards the pulsing depths of the distant Outaouais. Only a few days ago, the shrubs in the wetlands were a promise of greening; today, they burst into pussy willows tufts and carnelian dogwood fluff. Tree buds popped into tender, fluttering leaves. Emerald grass decorated each blade with sparkling dew. A gentle breeze sported the scents of flowing sap and fervent soil.

Daisy lolled between waking and dreaming, beside the paddock where the sheep nibbled tender morsels poking upwards from the rich, tepid mud.

However, her nap did not last long. The barn door opened with a clatter. Friday jumped into bounces, barking enthusiastically. The cat scrambled up a tree. Aster chattered with excitement, urgently tugging at Alie's bridle. The pony allowed herself to be hustled towards the riding ring by this little person bubbling with energy, decked out in riding helmet and cowboy boots.

"I brushed and brushed, but still I couldn't get all the winter fur off. And her mane—I just couldn't get the knots out. And her tail is full of burrs."

"It'll do for now," said Daisy, seasoned with many years of experience. She rolled onto her side and gathered herself to her feet with considerable effort. She was a far cry from the spry young girl who used to climb apple trees and spring onto the backs of galloping horses. "Her coat will shine up when summer gets here, and we'll get her trimmed up nicely before the fair. First things first. Let's see if you can ride the beast."

"I already know how to ride," said Aster with unsettling self-assurance. "I've read all about horses and horseback riding in books from the library."

"Yes, yes, that's good," said Daisy. "However, the pony hasn't read those books. She has her own ways of teaching. You'll see. Patience, patience."

Daisy had been reviewing the most important lessons that she needed to teach Aster. There was not a lot of time to prepare a child for riding in the Agricultural Fair Light Horse Show. Like most things worth learning in life, horseback riding was a skill that required years to master.

Daisy had taught riding for many years. She was well familiar with the traditional toes-up, heels-down approach. However, she also understood the nature of horses. She firmly believed that the lessons learned had little to do with formalities and everything to do with function. The horse world had many facets, ranging from the social elitism of the highest echelon to the backyard pony. Money could buy status, but not ability. Through the millennia of human history, horses had always been equalizers. Either a person could ride, or she could not.

Daisy studied the behaviour of the pony as the pair approached the riding ring. Daisy knew more about horses than she did about humans. She spent years tending to a pastured herd, observing the animals in their natural setting. By watching the horse, she could understand the character of the young person handling her mount. The scraggly Welsh pony had a glint in her eye, gritting her teeth against the bit in her mouth. The creature submitted to Aster's will, but only to a point. Eventually she would rebel against the girl's self-conceit. Always Christmas was still the boss.

The pony was crabby in principal, but with good reason.

Daisy knew a lot about school horses. Over the years, she frequently extolled the benefits of a good school pony to the parents of her riding students. Often her clients assumed cute, little horses were tiny pushovers that were easy to control, tolerant and willing. Daisy had been a conscientious riding instructor. She explained over and again that ponies taught humility. Small creatures had to be tough and quick to defend themselves. Ponies were hardy, bred to work all day and to survive on poor feed in the harshest climates.

Daisy would say, "They *are* good mounts for small children, but not because they are docile and submissive. On the contrary, ponies clearly set limits for children who are constantly testing to see what they can get away with. A pony's threshold for bad behaviour is very low. They are quick to react to mistreatment and very effective with their backlashes. A child has to learn to be patient and respectful in order to ride a pony well. A good coach monitors the balance so neither child nor pony gets the upper hand. Eventually, they must develop a mutual respect for each other's abilities. Horse and rider must learn to get along."

Aster was happily unaware of the pony's mood. "I explained everything to Alie in the barn when we were getting ready," she said as she marched past the spruce tree, dragging the pony behind her. "I intend to win a ribbon riding this pony in the fair."

Daisy did not bother to reply. She knew better. Some things were better left unsaid.

By the time Daisy reached the mounting block, Aster was already attempting to climb aboard.

"Whoa! Hold your horses," Daisy said, puffing to catch her breath. "You've forgotten some important steps. First of all, have you checked your girth?"

Aster's puzzled expression confirmed that she had not done so.

"You must always check the girth before you get on. Never rely on someone else to check your equipment. If the saddle slips under the horse's belly, you are the one who gets hurt. Take responsibility for your own safety—always."

Daisy showed her how to tighten the strap that held the saddle in place around the pony's ample belly. "Now what do you do?"

The child put one foot in the stirrup and clumsily mounted into the saddle. Her stirrups were longer than her legs, and both reins were on the same side of the horse's neck.

"Get down," Daisy said simply.

"Why do I have to? I just got on," Aster complained with a little girl's pout.

"Do as I say," Daisy spoke firmly, leaving no room for argument. "Now."

The child resisted. Daisy waited.

"I don't know how."

"Ah ha!" Daisy broke the stalemate, exclaiming with delight. "Now we're getting somewhere. Roll forward towards your belly. Swing the far leg over the rump, and then let yourself down to the ground slowly."

Aster forgot to sulk and did as she was told.

"Now I have your attention," Daisy said with enthusiasm. "We've just learned another very important lesson in life: never get yourself into a situation unless you have figured out beforehand how to get out of it—especially if you are on a moving animal capable of taking off in an instant at a mad gallop with you hanging on for dear life!"

Daisy rearranged the bridle and adjusted the stirrups to the proper length. "Now you can show me that perfect riding position you learned about in your book."

Aster climbed back into the saddle with more ease and assurance. She gathered up the reins and sat straight, looking between the pony's ears, her feet in the stirrups with heels down.

"Smile," Daisy said. "The judge will always give extra points for a pretty smile."

Aster's face lit with a smile that brightened her whole countenance, as if she suddenly became aware that all her dreams of riding had now come true for real.

"Now, that's a prize winner."

Praise from her mentor broadened the grin even more.

Daisy remembered the excitement, the thrill of her heart skipping a beat at the dream of winning first prize. The announcer would pause just before reading the judge's selection when all the riders were lined up, waiting for the decision. Each competitor reviewed the performance of the class, trying to decipher where the horse excelled, and when a rider made a mistake. The announcement blared over the microphone: "And the winner is ..." A hush would descend over the crowd. With throbbing heart, she would stroke her horse's neck gently, whispering, "You did your best." She believed her horse always performed to the utmost for her.

She had her share of prizes tucked away in boxes in the attic. However, when she began coaching, she realized each student performed to the limit, no matter what one's skill level. Whereas only one champion claimed the red, many strived to do their best. The world needed them all. Not everyone could be a winner, but each person, however young and however challenged, earned a special and unique place in the scheme of the universe.

The lesson proceeded gradually through the first steps of laying a foundation for good riding.

"Keep both legs on either side of the horse, with the horse between you and the ground." Daisy explained the art as she had learned to teach it best over the years. "Move as the horse moves."

The coach illustrated each skill with a practical exercise.

"Take your feet out of the stirrups. As the pony takes each step, feel the animal's body swaying beneath you. Sense the rhythm of the gaits. All horses have a perfect tempo. The walk is four beats; the trot, two; the canter three. Now, count the steps.

"Speak through your body. The horse understands through touch.

"Look where you're going. A horse sees through your eyes.

"Use your body to speak the language of muscles."

As the lesson progressed, Aster focussed more consistently. Her expressions were a kaleidoscope of emotions ranging from concentrated intensity to frustration, to joy in success when she finally mastered a skill. The pony was her mirror, instantly reflecting correct signals or mixed messages. Daisy interpreted.

"Watch her ears; you will know if she's listening. She quickened her step—you used too much heel. She will not stop if you pull too hard. She relaxed her neck when you softened your back."

The morning flew by. The little cat lounged on the fence, dodging the barn swallows dive-bombing just out of reach. Friday surveyed the activity curiously, until he realized the lesson was proceeding in circles; then he stretched out in a safe corner for another nap. He occasionally flicked an ear in response to an inflection in Daisy's voice, to be sure his assistance was not required. The sheep lazed in a huddle, chewing their cud. Flies buzzed in the fresh lawn. Bees hummed through the apple blossoms. Sparrows gathered feathers for their nests.

The pony went round and round, content that the pace of the lesson was not too demanding.

When they had covered most of the basics, Daisy said, "Eventually, something will happen. You will part ways with your mount. So let's practice that now."

"What? Practice what?"

"We're going to practice how to fall off."

"But I don't want to fall."

"Well, you may as well stop riding now," said Daisy with a shrug of the shoulders. "You cannot learn to ride without falling off. We say, 'You have to fall at least a hundred times before you're a real rider.' So you might as well learn how to do so correctly right from the beginning."

Daisy explained step-by-step how to perform an emergency dismount. "With both arms around the horse's neck, swing one leg over, land on two feet, cross the arms, tuck the body into a ball and roll away. Try it—slowly. Make sure it's correct the first time. Your brain will tell the body how to do this when you are in a hurry, when you don't have time to think about it."

Daisy held the pony at a standstill. Aster carefully repeated the steps as Daisy had explained them.

"Hug, land, tuck, roll."

The moment Aster landed on the ground, Friday ran to her, licking her face and jumping on her as she struggled to her feet.

"The most important rule about falling is this," Daisy continued with her hand on the pony's bridle. "If you fall, you must get back on immediately."

Aster brushed herself off, scratched Friday behind the ears, patted her pony's neck and proceeded to clamber back into the saddle. This time, she was agile and quick to mount.

They practiced the emergency dismount a few times until Daisy was satisfied that the child's reflexes were well-ingrained. "That's it for the day," she announced. "That was a very good lesson."

"Can't we do just one more thing?" Aster pleaded. "We haven't even trotted yet."

"The time to end a lesson is when you want to keep going," said Daisy. She repeated the lines as she had so many times before, when a young student had more energy than good sense. "You always want to end on a good note."

"Just one little trot?"

Daisy was already holding the gate open to make way for the entourage to return to the barn. "You still have to look after your horse. Take off the saddle and bridle. Brush your horse. Clean the tack. Put everything away. Don't forget to give your pony her treats before you turn her out. That's her favourite part of the whole day. A school pony needs to feel appreciated. You can't have a good ride without a happy horse."

By the time they returned to the kitchen for lunch, it was already mid-afternoon.

"My goodness, what a day we've had. How time flies when you're having fun."

Daisy prepared a hot vegetable soup and sandwiches. Aster was unusually quiet while they ate. Before Daisy served cookies for dessert, the little girl was sound asleep with her head cradled on her arm on the table.

Daisy prepared a strong cup of tea. She settled into her favourite rocking chair with her legs propped on a stool. The cooing of the dove lulled her to sleep as well.

Chapter 31

INTO THE EYE OF THE STORM

Emily had barely stepped inside the door of her apartment before the telephone was ringing. She hastily hung her coat in its place and rushed to answer. Poor Charlie did not even have time to wind himself around her ankles and demand treats.

"Mrs. Blossom?" said a voice that she could not quite recognize.

"Yes?"

"It's Toni."

She scanned her memory, trying to match the caller's tone to a face. "Yes?"

"The Curiosity Shoppe. You were here just the other day. You left your card. You told me to call in case I had news about the white boot fellow."

"Oh, yes," she said with sudden recognition. "How nice to hear from you!"

Antoine's words sounded strangely muffled by his hand over the receiver.

"He's here—the man you were asking about. He came back for the camouflage jacket."

"I'll be right there," Emily said in an urgent whisper, as if someone might overhear the conversation. Charlie merely cocked his furry head and commented on his empty stomach.

Emily grabbed her coat from its hook and rushed out the door, leaving her lonely cat mewling in vain.

When she arrived outside the store, Antoine was standing in the doorway. His delicate, bejewelled fingers flourished a cigarette outside. Wisps of smoke curled into the fresh air. He spoke over his shoulder to an unseen customer inside. Detective Blossom saw the black Jeep with a dented fender parked on the street. She recognized the getaway vehicle Pete had described as the one driven by the suspect on the night of the murder. Antoine gestured with an exaggerated nod of the head, indicating the man was about to leave the store.

With no hesitation, Emily slipped into the back of the Jeep and hid, out of sight behind the driver's seat. She congratulated herself on her quick thinking. The man emerged from the store, shopping bag in hand, and headed for his vehicle. Lucky for her, he threw the bag into the back over his shoulder without looking inside. He put the key in the ignition, and the Jeep roared to life.

Emily could just discern Toni's startled expression through the back window as the Jeep bore her away down Main Street.

Only when they were travelling through Hamilton Mills, towards the bridge across the Ottawa River to Quebec, did Emily begin to question what she had done. Upon reassessing her predicament, she came to several sickening conclusions: She was stowed away with a murderer. She had no idea of their destination. Not a soul knew where she was, and she had no cell phone. She had no explanation as to how she came to be there. There was no escape.

Emily speculated that in all probability, she would not return alive. She had only herself to blame. Thanks to her impulsive foolhardiness, her chances of survival were becoming slimmer by the second. She did not feel like such a clever sleuth after all. In fact, Aspiring Detective Emily Blossom suddenly felt dismally vulnerable and very alone.

After they crossed the bridge, Emily lost all sense of direction. From her hiding place on the floor, she could only see the sky and the lacy tops of trees speeding by. When the Jeep began to heave and jounce, she figured they had headed up the mountain into the back woods of the Gatineau Hills.

After what seemed like hours, the Jeep made an abrupt turn, and the road became even rougher. The shock absorbers had long since ceased to function. The vehicle lurched and jerked slowly towards their destination. Emily would not have been surprised if a fender or two ended up in a pothole along the way.

She sat on the floor with her back propped against the door. Her body had passed the point of pain. By now, every bone in her body had rattled loose from its socket. She was so firmly wedged behind the driver's seat that she could barely twitch a muscle. When they finally came to a halt, Emily did not even attempt to extricate herself from her hiding place. She could not move.

Her chauffeur threw the keys on the dashboard and heaved the door open. She heard his footsteps trudging across gravel to an unknown destination. Presently, she heard the steps returning.

Her door flew open. The man reached over her limp body to pick up the bag of clothes he had purchased at the Curiosity Shoppe. At the same time, the Jeep flooded with sunlight. When he discovered her, a low growl emanating from deep within his gut grew into a very loud exclamation.

"What the fuck?"

She did not know which one of them was more startled.

She said softly, "Hallo, there. Could you help me, please? I'm quite stuck. I'm afraid I cannot get out by myself."

With some tugging and pulling, he from the outside and she from her firmly wedged hideaway, they managed to free one limb and then another from confinement. There was much grunting and ouching in the process, but both humans were intent on resolving the conundrum as quickly as possible. Eventually, Emily was upright, swaying a bit as she held firmly onto the stranger's shoulder to restore her equilibrium. He towered above her but held her steady until she could stand on her own. Sensations gradually returned to her extremities.

"Who the fuck are you?" he said, recovering from the surprise of finding a little old lady lodged in the back of his car. "What the fuck are you doing here?"

Emily tut-tutted in her most disarming manner, somewhat like a broody hen soothing ruffled feathers. She calculated that she had one chance to curb his anger, to prevent him from killing her on the spot. She would use the shock factor to her advantage.

"Well, actually, I am an investigative journalist. I'm doing research on … Well, I'm looking into … I can explain everything."

She almost heard the wheels turning in her brain, searching for some kind of plausible explanation that would satisfy him. She needed a ploy that would lower his defences and put him off guard. She believed that deep down, everyone had a yearning to be recognized as being special, to be understood and accepted no matter how degraded that person had become.

As a stalling tactic, she proposed a distraction. "You wouldn't by any chance have a cup of tea?"

Thankfully, he complied with her request, and soon a pot of water was bubbling rapidly above a roaring campfire.

She smoothed her clothes and patted down her hair, taking stock of her appearance. Then she surreptitiously glanced around to see where she was. She felt quite incongruous in these surroundings.

A quick survey revealed a ramshackle hut made of bits of tin and rough-hewn logs, covered with bark and torn tarps. The campsite nestled in a clearing in the woods. A car seat and upholstered armchair, with stuffing protruding in all directions, appeared to be the only site for a cozy chat. Emily chose a perch and settled down.

"These primitive chairs are so quaint. This is a lovely setting for a cottage like yours. How lucky you are to have found such privacy amid such beauty!"

Her companion was not at ease with chatterers. He was a man of few words and less manners. Emily babbled, undeterred by his reticence.

"I hope I'm not interfering with your day. I admire your choice of decor," she said, pointing to a skull and crossbones made from an unfortunate, unidentifiable, former creature of the forest.

Eventually, her host produced a somewhat tattered box of Red Rose Orange Pekoe tea.

"This is the perfect tea for such an occasion." Emily clucked in her most congratulatory manner. Diplomatically, she did not ask for milk or sugar.

All the while, her mind was churning. How to introduce the gist of her interrogation? She could not come right out and ask him whether he was a murderer, and if so, why he had he committed such a dastardly act as to kill a man in cold blood. Where had he gotten deadly chemical weapons, of all things? Actually, she was unsure whether she really wanted to know the whole truth. Knowing the answers could be quite dangerous.

Her curiosity ran rampant. What would bring someone to live like this? Off by himself in the woods, subsisting on the bare minimum of comforts to survive? Why, in this day and age, would a person choose to live this way? What experiences would create such a mysterious human being? What nightmares haunted his dreams?

A detective must foster her imagination, without becoming personally involved with the criminal mind. Lines between justifiable actions and crime become blurred. However, in the face of danger, make the enemy a friend. Often the suspect will reveal more information voluntarily if conditions are conducive to confidentiality Successful detectives may cultivate a nurturing relationship of trust and caring. Offering friendship and empathy can be an effective defence against assault.

Chapter 32

BLOOD MOON

With her teacup nestled between her palms, Emily rested her elbows on her knees and stared into the flames. She began the conversation to put him at ease. To excuse her bad behaviour, she spoke like a little girl: a touch of whine and a lot of sweetness.

"I very much needed to talk with you. Hiding in your Jeep is the only way I could think of to track you down."

Her host nervously paced back and forth. Even on his home turf, he was out of his comfort zone. Expressions passed across his face like shadows over water. In succession, confusion, anger, fear, bewilderment, frustration and curiosity transformed one grimace into another. Emily could only imagine the conversation he carried on with himself in his head.

A wool toque shaded his eyes. His clothes were tattered. Several layers of colourful leggings, each of a different length, covered his pants, tucked from his boots up to his thighs. His coat, with patches over patches, bunched into his waistband secured by a canvas strap for a belt. Under all the padding, he was pitifully skeletal. Veins stood out on the back of his hands that trembled when he rolled cigarettes, one after another, from a crumpled package of tobacco stored in his jacket pocket. His fingers were orange with nicotine stains, and his claw-like fingernails were black with dirt.

For all his rough exterior, the man's eyes were soft; his manner was delicate and strangely feminine. Emily felt a tenderness towards him, as she would towards a wild animal caught in a trap. She began the conversation gently and apologetically.

"I want to get to know you. You're a very special person. I know you've been through a lot of hardship. Let me explain myself, so you know where I'm coming from. I'm writing an article on Canadian soldiers who recently fought overseas. I'm interested in Platoon VX. I understand you took part in their operations?"

The trapped animal inside this tortured man suddenly turned vicious. His eyes became slits of meanness; his muscles tensed, ready to pounce. Emily took a deep breath and continued calmly, well aware that the slightest mistake in her demeanour could bring instant death.

"How do you know about Platoon VX?" he hissed between his teeth.

Without appearing coy, Emily said, "I have a confidential source. I know it's hokey and hardly original, but I call him Deep Throat."

"Who is it? Let me at the asshole."

"I cannot reveal my sources." Emily smoothed her pants and folded her fingers in a knot.

"I'll tear him apart!"

"That won't be necessary." Then Emily decided to retract her approach and return from a different angle. "Mr. …? I don't believe we've actually met. Forgive me. I barge in here, take liberties coming to your home and sit down for a lovely cup of tea, and I haven't even introduced myself."

The glaring eyes softened just enough to encourage Emily to proceed.

"My name is Emily, Emily Bl—" Quickly Emily changed tack again, swallowing her words before she revealed too much. "Just call me Emily. That's fine."

He tilted his head sideways, listening.

She stood up and offered to shake his hand. "And you are?"

He wiped his hands on his pants. After slight hesitation, he returned a limp palm in response. "Call me Frankie."

She gasped. She had hit her mark. Ecstatically, she laid on lavish praise. "You wouldn't be Frankie Duval? The famous Frankie Duval? Are you really the champion fiddle player they still talk about in Scottsdale?"

She knew she had caught him off guard when the blood drained from his cheeks. He looked faint. His pale lips twitched into a reluctant smile, as if triggered into another life by distant memories.

"How do you know?" he asked.

To his trembling response, Emily became contrite.

"Just a lucky guess," she said with relief. "Now that we're on the same page, Frankie, sit down, and we'll have a good chat. This is quite a coincidence." She continued without allowing him the chance to ask too many questions. "I was just talking about you with Angus McInness. He remembers you fondly. Now, tell me all about yourself. I know it was a long time ago. What drew you to want to play the fiddle?"

His eyes glazed over as memories seemed to flood into his troubled brain.

"Tell me about the fiddle competitions. Who were some of the fiddlers you played with?"

His lips moved as if reciting a list of fallen comrades.

"Mostly locals. We called them the Macs—lots of MacDonalds. Alexander Clare MacDonald, Alexander Duncan MacDonald, Allan Joseph MacDonald. They were all cousins. Then there were the MacLeods and the MacGillivaries, the MacRaes and the McCormicks.

"Me and Jack—Jack Blossom—we were from the north, the next county up the road. Jack was English, blond hair, blue eyes and white as they come. I was French, dark skin, tall and straight black hair. They called me Blackie behind my back."

"How did you learn to play so well?"

"From our fathers, who learned from their fathers, and their fathers before them. We could count our generations back to the early settlers. The Macs came from Scotland. Jack's folks were Loyalists who came to Canada after the American Revolution. My family came over on the boat with Sam Champlain and mixed with the aboriginals who were already here."

"Did you play the same style of music?"

"Fiddle made us equal. The tunes were different. Either you could play, or you couldn't. Everybody likes to dance; whether to a jig or a reel, it's all the same. At the dances, the music would take off. Your feet got to tapping and stepping. A waltz was always a good excuse to hold your sweetheart close and whirl around the floor. Jack and I could get them going pretty good. Not too many would sit still when we got to playing together."

"Were you and Jack Blossom good buddies?"

"We were kids. We cut up and made up, fought over the girls. What else is new? Like any teenagers."

"Then what happened?" Emily prompted.

"There was this girl, Carly MacLeod. She was sweet on me, but Jack liked her too. She was different, real pretty, but kind of screwy. She could change moods in a flash. One minute she was madly in love; the next she hated your guts. She could never make up her mind. After I won the championship, she asked me to play for her step dancing competition. Jack's nose was out of joint, and so he left and never came back. He always was a pushover and never stood up for himself. Funny that he ended up in the military, really."

"What do you mean?"

"He wasn't much of a fighter."

As Frankie told his side of the story, Emily became more confused. Her theories were losing ground. She'd assumed that Frankie was Jack's murderer. She'd conjectured that Frank Duval, the assassin, had sought revenge for an argument from years past. Perhaps a triangle love affair originating from their teenage years had gone horribly wrong.

Emily had to reconsider. Frankie's version of the past was at odds with what she knew. However, more important, his tone and his attitude were inconsistent. This vagabond did not speak like a man consumed with burning hatred. True, he might be absolutely mad—in which case, he had become very adept at hiding certain aspects of his criminal personality. On the other hand, he could simply be living in a dream world of his own imagination, with no fear of the consequences of his actions.

In any case, Emily felt there would be a logical explanation if she could only persuade him to continue to confide in her. To do this, she must remain unobtrusive, interjecting only when necessary to keep his story on track. Too much pushing or insisting would blow her cover wide open. It could all end in disaster one way or another.

"What happened to Carly?"

"Oh, that. Didn't work out. At first things seemed right. We thought we were in love. We moved in together. We had a good thing going. But that all fell apart. We both had our own baggage.

"Even though we were just kids barely out of high school, she had some screwy idea about getting married. She thought we would have a huge wedding, invite all the folks and their long-lost relatives. She would be the beautiful bride in white with a handsome, devoted husband. She pictured herself as the happy housewife with four lovely children. I would settle down, get a job and come home every night to my little woman.

"Only trouble was, she was never happy a day in her life. She always wanted what she could not have. Now, I realize she was probably suffering from depression, or she was bipolar. Plus, I was all fucked up. It wasn't a good combination. Thank God we never did have kids."

He crouched in front of the fire with his chin cradled on his entwined fingers. The light of the flames flickered in his dark eyes. At some point, he rolled himself a joint. The sweet smell of marijuana floated above the camp.

He offered Emily a toke. She debated only an instant before accepting the spliff. Although she had never smoked dope before, she dared not refuse. She inhaled deeply, as she had seen others do. Immediately she regretted her enthusiasm. Her throat burned, her eyes watered and she erupted into a fit of coughing.

Frankie barely acknowledged her distress, so intent was he on reminiscing. He reached over the fire for the joint that she happily returned to him, refusing the offer of another toke.

As soon as Emily recovered her breath, she asked, "You seem like a normal sort of guy. What baggage do you have?"

He chuckled without smiling. Then he took a deep drag and studied the smoke as it furled from his nostrils. His eyes were red; his pupils were dilated.

"Let's just say in my family, there was no difference between sex and love. A kid could get it in the ass from one adult, and end up beaten to a pulp for telling. Trust was not exactly a word in my vocabulary. When I was about 10 or 11, all my tears turned to anger. I learned to hate my parents for what they did to me. I hated my whole family for looking the other way. How was I supposed to love and cherish some fragile, beautiful girl who didn't have a clue about reality? It wasn't going to happen."

"Is that when you left home?"

"I followed Jack's example: I joined the Canadian forces and enlisted to go overseas. I had no idea I'd end up in the same platoon as Corporal Jack Blossom. What were the chances of that? Anyway, it turned out okay. He was a decent officer, and we got along."

"Are you telling me you and Jack Blossom got back together and renewed your friendship when you were in the army?"

Frankie glanced at her, triggered by her tone of disbelief. He didn't appear threatened, only misunderstood. "You don't get it," he said. He studied her expressions, measuring the extent of her ability to comprehend. "Nobody could know what it's like over there, unless you've been in a war zone. The rules are different. Death has no value. Life has no value. You shoot to kill, or you get killed. It's as simple as that."

"Is that what Platoon VX was all about?"

At this point, Frankie stood up and began to pace again. His face flushed, and he sputtered through broken teeth. "I don't know where you heard that shit. That information is totally confidential. Nobody knows about VX—nobody. We were all sworn to secrecy."

"What does VX actually stand for?"

"Who the hell knows?" He flailed his arms in a gesture of frustration. His spit hissed in the campfire. At this point, he was yelling. The veins stood out in his neck, and his eyes bulged. "It was invented in Britain in the 1950s as a pesticide. Then, go figure: in concentrated doses, they figured out it killed humans too! Whoop-dee-do!"

"How can that be?"

"It's a chemical compound. The deadliest weapon of mass destruction ever invented. You should see what happens when it's used in battle. On second thought, I wouldn't wish that on my worst enemy. It instantly suffocates any living creature it comes in contact with. Insects, livestock, humans—they all die the same way, in horrible contortions of pain. I've seen the devastation in Northern Iraq. Bodies all over the place. Men, women and children, all their pets, even the vermin in the gutters—all dead."

"What were you doing in Northern Iraq? I thought you were with the Canadian Forces. They never fought on the ground in the Middle East."

"Don't kid yourself. Ever heard of JTF2? It's a special operations regiment tasked with counterterrorism operations."

"But chemical weapons of mass destruction? Those have been banned."

"Lady, I don't know what planet you live on. There are millions of gallons of toxic chemicals, manufactured for use in war, stored in the good ol' US of A. There's so much of the stuff that nobody knows how to get rid of it all. Do you honestly think they went to all the trouble and expense to make that crap for nothing?"

"Why don't we know about this?"

"Go on the Web. You'll find all sorts of information you don't want to know about. Mind you, most of the weapons—including guns, tanks and chemicals—are sold to the enemy."

"To the enemy? Why would anyone do that?"

"Money," he replied.

"I beg your pardon?"

"It's good for the economy."

Emily shook her head. "No! That's absurd."

Frankie gave up, melting onto his seat. He buried his head in his hands, with his palms over his eyes. Presently, he looked at her. She thought he might have been weeping. His voice relayed defeat and despair.

"The whole world is absurd. Let me tell you a little story about these terrorists. We got a call from a woman in the remote desert. She was crying and pleading with us. She said, 'Send the planes. This is our location. We want you to bomb us all.'

"When the dispatcher questioned her further to get the exact location, she gave him the information in detail. Then she said, 'I'm here with 250 women. I've been raped 60 times already today. Please save us. Kill us all. We have nothing to live for.'"

Emily felt as if she had been kicked in the stomach. She had not bargained for such blatant truth. Senseless rage, brutal violence, even heartless revenge—she could fathom all that. She had been prepared to face an evil man who deserved to be punished in the court of law. However, not this. She could not imagine living through the experience of such horror in real life. She realized how protected and safe she was from the true cruelty of humankind. Her concepts of good and justice had become quite undone. There were no clear lines of black on one side and white on the other. How could she have been so naive?

Still, she had to continue her interrogation. She needed to pursue the full story to the end. "What about Jack?" she said in a whisper. "What happened to Jack?"

Frankie's face was ashen; his lips were pursed. Sorrow consumed every fleeting expression of hope. "Before we were discharged from our duties, I stole vials of VX. Just in case, we agreed … just in case …"

"In case of what?"

She knew she would never be able to erase the look he gave her. His torture burned into her memory like a scar. His story came from another dimension of the past, one that she'd sensed but had never encountered.

"I had the automatic weapon. Jack stood by my shoulder. We were waiting for an enemy soldier to make a mistake. All he had to do was to show his face around the corner of a building where we knew he was hiding. I'm the sniper; my aim is deadly accurate. Our nerves are shot. We've been awake for three days and nights, with no sleep and hardly anything to eat." His gaze froze on her face. "This was our last mission before leaving for home."

With the violence of an explosion, Frankie burst into sobs. He wailed like a small child, as if releasing every pain he had ever experienced into the silent, looming forest around them. He moaned and beat his chest with clenched fists. He howled like a wolf at the full moon.

With shivers running up and down her spine, Emily waited silently in the shadows of the lengthening day. She knew he had to let it all out before he would be ready to continue his tale to its tragic end. She could do nothing to mitigate his grief. She had no confidence to attempt wheedling her way to a resolution; there was no easy escape. She had to wait him out. When he had no more energy, he resumed his account as if mesmerized, with a musical lilt to his telling.

"All of a sudden, this little girl comes running out of the house with a kitten in her arms. She's crying and holding a little ball of fluff against her dress. She is barefoot and dressed in rags, with her hair straggling in every direction. I can describe every detail of what she looked like, how she hugs that kitten to her chest, how she calls for her father to help her. He sticks his head out from behind the wall, and I blow him to pieces. Then I turn the gun on the child and obliterate her too. The kitten scampers away, and my bullets send its fuzzy body flying into red bits in the dust. Jack is screaming at me to stop, but I can't. Once I pull the trigger, my fingers seize on the grip. When the ammunition runs out, there isn't a living creature in sight. I remember the awful, dead stillness. Only the breeze blows wafts of sand whooshing over the dunes like echoes of sadness."

Together, surrounded by the forest, Emily and Frankie waited for the sounds of the present to wash over them: the campfire crackling, a tree branch falling, leaves rustled by a gentle breeze. For a second, or an hour, they lost track of time until somehow the torturing memories faded into the quiet peace around them. Only then could Frankie resume his story.

"After that, Jack and I made a pact. When we could no longer live with the nightmares. We would use the vials. Eventually, death soothes all wounds."

A bird chirped in a tree overhead.

Emily thought she heard the motor of a truck in the distance, slowly making its way up the mountain.

"Is that what happened that night at the magic show?"

"Jack knew I was coming. He wanted to hide in plain sight. He was always the one to back down first. He was such an idealist. When it came to the crunch, he didn't have the stomach for the real thing."

"Why in front of an audience, surrounded by a hundred people?"

"Safety in numbers." Frankie chuckled. Then he looked at her with his sad, ancient eyes. "He wanted to give the kid a chance to fly to freedom, where she would be safe. He didn't want her to see his death. He had it all planned out. How the ambulance would take time to arrive, how the doctors would not suspect the cause of death, how the cops would be slow to figure out who he was and where he lived. She would be long gone by the time anyone guessed what had really happened."

By now, they both recognized the sound of an approaching vehicle.

"And you?" she asked him.

"I'm not quite ready yet," he said. "I still have one more matter of business to take care of. Then I'll know it's time."

The Pickin' Truck bounced into the clearing with gears grinding and fenders rattling. The brim of the driver's hat barely cleared the steering wheel. Pete Picken held his pipe between the gaps in his teeth. A wisp of smoke curled from the window. Without turning off the motor, he waited with his hands on the steering wheel. They could see him hesitate. Emily took the cue.

"My ride's here." She shook hands with the murderer. "Well, Frankie Duval, I don't know what to say. Thank you for telling me your side of the story. It has been a privilege to know you."

Then she flung her arms around his lean body. Her hug was strong and sincere. His body was so frail beneath the layers of rags, she feared she would break him with the slightest pressure. Then, before leaving, she gently put her hand against his cheek and stared into the depths of his eyes. She gazed as if into an endless night sky.

"No man should have to live with such tortured memories," she said. "I cannot tell you how sorry I am for your pain."

Then she turned and walked towards Pete's truck with slow and concentrated steps. She knew there was no turning back.

The exhausted detective climbed into the truck and nestled into the passenger seat. Without a word, Pete navigated the turnabout and headed back down the mountain. The monastery appeared in a distant valley like a dark beacon.

Emily allowed her head to loll back against the headrest. She turned her face towards the window.

"How did you know how to find me?" Her voice trembled.

"I know this country like the back of my hand," he said. "Been picking antiques up here for years. I make it my business to know what goes on."

Tears filled her eyes and trickled down the wrinkles of her cheeks. "You know, Pete," she said hoarsely, "you are the most wonderful man in the world. I do love you dearly."

"Yeah, yeah," he said, studying the rutted road from beneath the brim of his hat.

The truck jostled, hole to hole, down the rutted road.

By the time they reached the pavement, crossing the bridge to Ontario, Emily Blossom was sound asleep.

Chapter 33

STELLAR SINGULARITY

The day of the fair was a gift of sunshine. Aster woke Daisy at four in the morning so they could get all the chores done before leaving the farm for the day.

"And the pony. Don't let me forget the pony," Daisy said. "I did that once. I'll tell you that story once we're on our way."

They bustled about, crossing each item off their list as they loaded equipment onto the trailer.

"Remember the rule about breakfast. We'll go in and have a bite before leaving. No matter how nervous you are, you need a good breakfast for energy. Sometimes you won't get to eat again until the show is over."

The pony knew the routine, even though years had passed since she was an active show pony. She loaded with only the smallest of protests, just to ensure she would get her reward of carrots once she was on the trailer. From the driver's seat, Daisy could see her dog's reflection in the side-view mirror. Friday watched them pull out of the barnyard with longing eyes. The white cat looped her tail around his nose affectionately, as if to soothe his aching heart.

As they pulled out of the driveway, Daisy ran through the list for the umpteenth time. "Are you sure you have your boots? Riding helmet? Show jacket? Did we bring an extra girth and reins? Water bucket, wash bucket, grooming kit?"

The truck slowly accelerated, pulling its precious cargo towards the fairgrounds. In the passenger seat, Aster was surprisingly thoughtful for a beginner. Daisy wondered how the child could sit so still on such an exciting day.

"Tell me how you forgot your horse," Aster said.

Daisy was happy to comply. A good yarn was a great antidote to calm the show jitters.

"We were going to a show down in Scottsdale that day," Daisy began. "As usual, we had a bunch of kids and ponies signed up for the first class. There's always a rush to get into the ring at the beginning of the day. I was also going to show my horse, Come by Chance, but our classes for advanced levels were in the afternoon.

"We loaded all the tack and counted the kids, helmets, boots and show clothes. We put the horses on the trailer, and off we went. We were halfway there when I remembered: I forgot to load my own horse! We had to go all the way back home to pick him up."

"Then what happened?"

"We made it, barely. The first class was showmanship. Some of the ponies looked a bit scruffy, and a couple of the kids had to tuck their hair up underneath the hats without braids."

"Did they win?"

"I don't actually remember," said Daisy, scratching her head. "Usually the older kids get the ribbons. They have more experience. The most important thing is to have a good time. That's what it's all about. You do your best. Just getting into the ring is sometimes the biggest challenge."

"I hope I win a ribbon," said Aster.

"Well, I wouldn't count on it," said Daisy. "Don't get your hopes up too high. If it's too easy, it's probably not worth doing. Just have fun with your pony. That way, she'll enjoy her day out, and you will both look forward to spending time together no matter what you're doing. That's the best way to be a winner."

"Did you and Come by Chance win ribbons?"

Daisy couldn't help but smile. "Chance was the best jumper I ever had. All I had to do was point him at a jump, and he'd sail over it. We beat the pants off some of those fancy hunters from the snooty barns."

"Do you have any ribbons?"

"We won our share."

Daisy realized she had stepped into a trap, but it was too late to back track now. She had forgotten that children were sponges. Young minds absorbed more by example than by speeches.

"The ribbons are in a drawer somewhere. It's the memories that count. You will remember today for the rest of your life. It's your first show; savour every minute."

When they arrived at the show grounds, trucks and trailers surrounded the barns, vying for the best spots closest to the ring. Small children with scruffy ponies in tow searched earnestly for preoccupied parents. Leggy hunters sported hundreds of tight braids and shiny saddles. Riders with polished boots and pearly smiles carelessly guided their mounts through crowds of inattentive visitors.

Daisy parked in a remote corner away from the hustle and excitement of the crowds. Sooner or later, they would have to enter the fray, but establishing a quiet corner of refuge usually made the day less onerous. Already the announcer was calling the first class.

"All competitors in Class Number 1 Open Showmanship should be in the collecting ring. The class begins in 15 minutes."

Daisy had chosen showmanship for Aster's first class. Although one of the most difficult to win, this category was open to competitors at all levels. Exhibitors ranked according to their tidy appearance and horsemanship on the ground; no riding was required. The judge assessed the cleanliness of horse and handler, the horse's behaviour and cooperation and the exhibitor's ability to follow patterns. For a beginner, this class was well-suited for gaining experience. The pony also had a chance to get used to the ring and the surroundings.

"Remember, walk like a princess," said Daisy. "Head high, walk proud, back straight. And don't forget that winning smile."

As they approached the in gate, Daisy scanned the crowd for familiar faces. She knew many of the horse crowd from the old days. Today, she hoped that Emily and Pete would be on hand to cheer on Aster. She reminded herself that the day was still young. They would probably make their appearance in time for the walk-trot class in the afternoon.

Daisy, the groom, made her last-minute touches. She tucked a wayward strand of hair under Aster's helmet and placed a dangling bridle strap into its keeper. Coach Daisy then whispered in her student's ear, "Avoid the horses with red ribbons in their tail—they kick. Steer clear if they start to bunch up. Find your spot, and keep your distance. Alie will look after you." Just before the child entered the ring, she called out, "Remember to have fun!"

A broad smile lit up Aster's face as she proudly led the pony right in front of the judge.

After finding a good vantage point just beside the announcer's stand, Daisy counted the competitors as they filed through the gate. Thirty-one well-dressed exhibitors paraded with shining horses through the dust. She stood leaning her elbows on the top rail of the fence, one foot propped on the bottom rail. Already in the early morning, the sun beat down on her. Luckily, she had remembered her broad-rimmed straw hat and sunglasses. Sunburn at horse shows was a common hazard.

"Well, if it isn't Daisy Blossom! I didn't believe I'd ever see you at one of these goddamn boring events again. How long has it been? A good 10 or 15 years, no?"

The fake British accent grated Daisy's nerves as quickly as it used to in the old show days. When she glanced over her shoulder, she hardly recognized Caroline Ballard for all her age spots and dyed pink hair.

"You don't look a day older," said Caroline in her sticky sweet, nasal accent.

Daisy recognized Caroline's fabrication, but she politely provided the proper response, "Neither do you."

Caroline tittered.

Both women knew they were lying. They always played an unspoken game of pretending to be someone they weren't.

They used to show against one another. Daisy remembered all too well how Caroline had perfected the art of crowding Daisy and Chance against the rail in the pleasure classes. With her overweight, nasty-tempered mare, Caroline forced her competitors to break stride right in front of the judge. If she won less than second prize, she would throw the ribbon in the mud as she left the ring.

Putting it mildly, Caroline Ballard was not exactly one of Daisy's favourite people.

"Isn't that the Blossom child with your old pony, Always Christmas?" Although Caroline pretended to have British blood, her nasal twang betrayed her Canadian origins, just like her grey hairs betrayed her age. "She looks just like her father did when he would come with you to the fair in the old days. I thought you had retired from that rat race. The pony must be ancient."

"Ponies live forever," said Daisy, defending her right of return.

They chatted as the exhibitors guided their horses around the ring. With each circuit, the pace became slower. Riding boots and polished hooves shuffled through the dirt. By the time 31 horses and handlers had lined up at the end of the arena, the youngsters were becoming restless. Their competitors' numbers slipped off to one side, the reins drooped, the shoulders slouched and attention waned. One by one, they led their horse away from the lineup, attempted to trot the horse in front of the judge and then returned into place to wait for the others to have their turn.

Daisy refused to respond to any more of Caroline's impertinent comments. She pretended to have been stricken by a sudden onset of elder deafness.

By the time Aster's turn came up, the princess had transformed to a waif, and the pony was fed up. When Aster stepped out of line, the pony refused to follow. Trotting was out of the question. Alie refused to halt in front of the judge and then dragged her handler towards the gate. When they finally returned to their place in line, the horse beside them, with a red ribbon in its tail, lashed out. In spite of her size, Alie returned the affront. Horses went flying in all directions. Children squealed, parents ran to the rescue and five exhibitors were excused from the ring before the class could proceed.

Aster's helmet was askew, and her eyes were blazing. Daisy recognized familiar telltale signs of dashed hopes displayed in the child's puffy bottom lip and knitted eyebrows. The girl was gearing herself up for a serious pout. Daisy met her at the gate and reached for the pony's reins while putting her arms around Aster's shoulders. She whispered so no one could hear.

"The pony saved your life," she said. "Did you see how she put herself between you and that ugly nag?"

Aster perked up. "She did?"

"She's small, but she wasn't going to let that horse kick you. We'll take her back to the trailer and make sure she's okay. Nobody got hurt. It could have been much worse."

Aster threw her arms around Alie's neck. Daisy boosted the child onto the pony's back, and together they returned to the trailer to recoup and re-energize for the next round.

Chapter 34

TWINKLE, TWINKLE, LITTLE STAR

The morning wore on.

"Horse shows are all about 'Hurry up and wait,'" Daisy said.

After the excitement of the first class, Daisy sat on the runner of the trailer, napping in the sun. Aster never tired of sitting bareback on Alie's back. The pony grazed, her whiskered muzzle locating every tender morsel of grass she could find. She flicked her skin when flies landed on her coat. She twitched her ear at the sound of a familiar voice.

"Whenever you get tired of watching the pony, I'll take over," said Daisy. "You can wander around the fairgrounds and see what else is going on. I'll be right here."

"I'm happy to stay with Alie," Aster said. "We'll go over there where the grass is longer."

Daisy floated in and out of consciousness, accustomed as she was to waiting for the progression of classes to proceed. She never understood why horse show committees scheduled the children's short stirrup classes later in the day. Making kids wait was cruel and unusual punishment, but some things never changed.

Much to her dismay, the sound of Caroline Ballard's voice interrupted her snooze. "Some horses should be banned from showmanship classes."

Daisy sat up and shook her head. She mumbled some platitude while she tried to think of a way to get rid of her intruder. Unfazed, Caroline apparently had an agenda.

"Last year, that same horse kicked a young teenager. She ended up at the hospital with a broken ankle. How about your girl? She didn't get hurt, did she?"

"Everything is okay. Kids are tough. Ponies are even tougher."

Daisy almost thought Caroline had mellowed—until her characteristic nasty streak revealed itself with the next comment.

"Your pony has always been a troublemaker, hasn't she?" said Caroline. She then continued without giving Daisy a chance to defend herself. "Do you remember when we would come to the shows with a whole herd of ponies, and 30 or 40 riding students? Why did we do that? We must have been gluttons for punishment."

Daisy growled under her breath. "We had good times. I wouldn't have done it any other way."

"And here you are again. What on earth are you thinking?" said Caroline.

Daisy could tell that Ms. Ballard was finally coming to the point of her chat. This woman always had an opinion, and she always shared her views with anyone she could bully. Daisy made a good target; she did not usually speak up.

"That poor child is an orphan now, isn't she?"

Daisy glanced over her shoulder to make sure Aster was out of hearing range. "I don't see that the girl's welfare is any of your business."

"It is horrible what happened to her father. Imagine, a murder right here in Emerald Hill! Have you ever heard of such a thing?"

Daisy asked, "How do you know what happened to Jack?"

"Well, the word is all around town, Dearie. Of course, you can't keep things like that a secret. After all, he was a local boy. Everybody remembers him when he lived down in the hollows and went to school here in town."

Daisy could feel the blood rising in her cheeks. Her head was pounding, and she could hardly keep her voice under control. "Caroline Ballard, you are a nosy body, and you should mind your own business!"

"Yes, well, I heard that Children's Welfare is going to be taking over the case. I just thought you'd want to know. Surely you're not planning on keeping the child with you."

"What if I was?"

"You're an old lady, Daisy Blossom," said Caroline, with a haughtiness that curdled Daisy's stomach. "Surely you don't think you could—"

"That's enough," Daisy said sternly. "I've had enough of you and your 'surely' this and 'old lady' that. Get out!" With outstretched arm, Daisy pointed a finger towards the barn. By this time she was shouting in spite of herself. "Leave me alone! And don't *ever* speak to me again! You never did know how to mind your own business, and you can go to the devil—the sooner, the better!"

She turned her back on Caroline and gave her the silent treatment until the woman understood that she had nothing more to say. Then Daisy watched those Ballard hips waddle back across the parking lot towards the horse barns.

Finally, after so many years of anguish, she had been able to tell Caroline just what she thought of her. She felt good, but her relief was short-lived.

The pony was tied to the trailer, and Aster was nowhere in sight.

Daisy quickly concluded that the child had overheard the whole conversation. The weight of disclosure came pounding down on her. She realized that she had been protecting both herself and Aster Blossom from the inevitable truth of her father's disappearance. Jack Blossom was dead. Aster was an orphan, alone and defenceless. Except for Daisy, nothing protected the child from the arbitrary whims of the world. She had managed to avoid dealing with the problems they faced together. They had not spoken a word of love or promises. Now the girl was gone, fleeing into the unknown with no one to comfort her. Daisy was beside herself with worry. This was a tragedy beyond her abilities to cope.

Chapter 35

SUPERNOVA

Emily and Pete strolled across the field towards Daisy's trailer. Emily was thoroughly enjoying the country setting of a real agricultural fair. A person could wear anything and still be in style: farmers in coveralls, teenagers with mini-skirts and flip-flops, children in strollers covered in cotton candy. No one paid any attention except to enjoy the activities and festive atmosphere. Besides, Emily took advantage of the excuse of uneven footing to thread her arm through Pete's and to lean on him, ever so slightly.

"I imagine that Daisy and Aster will be tending to the pony, preparing for the next class," said Pete.

However, when Emily did catch sight of Daisy, she was alone and very obviously looked a mess.

"Something's gone wrong," said Emily. "She's hysterical."

Flailing her arms, the distraught Daisy Blossom ran towards them, frantically waving, sputtering tears and sobs and gasping for breath.

"Aster's gone! She knows about her father! She's run away! Oh, please help me find her before something awful happens."

"Calm down, Daisy," Pete said in a tone that commanded attention. "Get a hold of yourself. You're going to have a heart attack, and then what help will you be? Get a grip."

Emily guided her sister-in-law back to the trailer and made her sit down until she could catch her breath. "There, there. You'll be all right." She tried to sound positive, even though she was close to losing every shred of patience she had left.

"I'm sure she overheard my conversation with that hateful Ballard woman," Daisy wailed. "I never would have let it go that far if I had known Aster was close enough to overhear. The girl wasn't ready to hear the truth!"

"What truth?" said Emily. "About what?"

"The truth about her father's murder. We were so protected down at the farm. We were safe. Now … Oh, Emily, how will we ever explain?"

While Emily tried to soothe Daisy's nerves, Pete stood nearby, surveying the crowd. The pony munched hay, eyeing the goings on with curiosity. She nuzzled Daisy's cheek and blew warm kisses against her skin. Eventually, Daisy was calm enough to explain the sequence of events leading up to Aster's disappearance.

"We'll fan out," said Emily. "She can't go too far."

"The place is packed. How are we going to find her?"

"I'll check out the women's bathrooms and the exhibit hall. Pete will pass through the carnival and the rides. Daisy, you wait here. She probably just went for a walkabout. When she realizes she has nowhere else to go, she'll come back. What's she wearing, Daisy?"

Daisy described Aster's show clothes. "She has brown riding boots and a short-sleeved riding shirt. She did have braids, but they've all fallen loose. Look for the freckles."

Leaving Daisy fretting but calmer now, Emily could hardly keep up with Pete's quick stride. Usually he sauntered; however, they were both infected with Daisy's fear. Emily trotted along beside him, chattering her thoughts aloud.

"We have to imagine how a child would react. Where would she go?"

They passed through the collecting ring, where riders practiced over jumps in helter-skelter fashion that seemed to have no particular order.

"It's amazing that they don't collide into each other."

Pete grabbed Emily's arm as they passed the giant tractors and combines on display. At first Emily thought he was being gentlemanly, but he pointed towards a vehicle parked on the road along the fence. Her heart skipped a beat when she realized he was looking at a black Jeep with Quebec license plates.

"Isn't that your friend's getaway vehicle?"

"It does look familiar. I don't imagine there are many like that one around. What would Frankie Duval be doing here?"

"I'm not sure we want to find out," said Pete. "There are lots of possibilities for creating a disaster, with all these people gathered in one spot."

"You don't think …?"

"I don't think. I'm just sayin', we're sitting ducks for a terrorist."

"I don't think Frankie would …" Emily could not finish her sentence. She did not want to imagine the consequences if she were wrong. "Let's split up. Time's running out."

The children's pet parade was underway in front of the grandstands. A little girl in a pink dress clutched a miniature poodle in her arms.

Both had matching pink hair bows and pink nail polish. One little boy wearing coveralls had a painted turtle in a box. A lad of about 10 hauled a reluctant calf behind him. Children proudly displayed their rabbits, guinea pigs and hamsters before the judges. The prickly hedgehog seemed a bit hard for its owner to manage.

Emily scanned the crowd. She saw a tall man dressed like a giant carrot walking hand in hand with a woman with curly blonde hair and dressed in farmer's coveralls and a straw hat. A child dressed in a clown suit with a Technicolor wig rode a green painted horse. She saw men in top hats, women in short shorts and children carrying enormous teddy bears—people of all description. However, she did not see Aster anywhere.

After checking out the washrooms and exhibit hall, she was on her way past the high-wire stunt tower when she spotted the petting zoo. This seemed a logical destination for a young girl who loved animals.

She was heading in that direction when she heard sirens in the distance. Five police cars, with lights flashing, turned into the fairgrounds entrance and skidded to a stop in front of the office. Constables tumbled out of their cruisers with guns drawn. Emily recognized Inspector Allard. She was about to change course to find out what he was doing when she remembered the immediacy of her mission. She had to find Aster. Her steps quickened.

Under a sign that read "Barney's Petting Zoo, Home of Happy Critters," a young girl was feeding the llama. Her hair straggled over her shoulders, and she wore brown cowboy boots. Standing beside her was a tall, dark fellow dressed in a camouflage jacket and tattered leggings. Emily recognized Frankie Duval immediately. He was talking to Aster Blossom.

Emily tried to call out, but she was too far away. As she began to run towards them, a group of teenagers with cotton candy and popcorn jostled her.

"Hey, lady," one of them jeered. "Watch where you're goin'!"

Emily ran in slow motion. Her feet could not move quickly enough to close the distance between her and the scene unfolding before her.

She helplessly observed a pantomime playing out in slow motion, across a chasm of gay fairgoers.

Frankie squatted down to address to Aster eye to eye. Emily could see that their lips moving in conversation. The girl's smile was soft and unafraid. In response to something he showed her in his hand, she turned her back to him and lifted her hair away from her shoulders. The stranger fitted a necklace around her delicate neck. He had difficulty with the clasp, and his fingers trembled. The child looked down at the pendant shining at her throat.

The necklace gleamed like a cluster of twinkling stars.

The delicate child embraced the ragged, desperate man.

Time stopped for an instant, as if it would endure forever.

Then the man turned and strode quickly into the crowd lined up for the rides.

Daisy ran up to Emily from behind, huffing and puffing. She pushed past her and hurried towards Aster, who gazed after the stranger who had disappeared into the dark.

Emily overheard her tell Daisy all about the tall stranger.

"He was my father's friend. He gave me this star pendant. He said it was a gift from my father. He said he hoped one day I would know the difference between rhinestones and diamonds."

Daisy hugged the child, wiping away her own tears with her sleeve. "Let's go back to look after the pony," she said.

Chapter 36

FINAL ECLIPSE

Familiar faces began to converge on the scene.

Pete veered towards the ticket booth, where a man sold tickets for the rides. Inspector Allard gathered his crew of constables around him and began shouting orders. Police officers scattered, running in all directions into the crowd. By now, a bunch of curiosity seekers began to gather at the gate to the Ferris wheel.

Multicoloured lights blared and blinked. Music blared from several loudspeakers spread throughout the grounds. Announcers called out across the field with the results of the competitions unfolding in every corner of the fairgrounds. Hawkers beckoned: three balls for a dollar, guaranteed to win a prize. Girls carried giant teddy bears and blue ponies won for them by their muscle-shirted boyfriends. Parents dragged and scolded wide-eyed children gaping at temptations bombarding them from every corner.

Emily witnessed the frenzy without comprehension.

Then she spotted him, high above the chaotic scene below: a ghostly silhouette against the dark sky, his angular facial features lit from below. Frankie Duval rode the Ferris wheel to the top. With arms splayed and crying out in joy, he bellowed above the din.

"Death is victory!"

He grasped a crimson scarf in one hand and emptied the contents of a vial onto the cloth. He covered his nose and mouth for an instant, and then he collapsed onto the chair, swinging high above the crowd.

A hush fell on the people watching from below. Slowly the lights of the Ferris wheel began to turn. The swinging seat squeaked, rocking with the heavy weight of a slumped body, hanging over the safety bar. By the time the chair reached the bottom of the platform, Frankie Duval was dead.

Constables leapt into action, pushing everyone aside and demanding space. Two figures in white haz-mat suits raced towards the Ferris wheel. One wore black high-heeled shoes, the other had black patent leather loafers without a speck of dirt on them. Soon an ambulance with sirens blaring and lights flashing pulled onto the grounds. The first responders handled the body with ultimate care. This time, they were alert to the dangers of chemical toxicity. The crowd parted as the stretcher carried away the body.

Soon people dispersed, and a hush descended on the scene. Gentle breezes swept across the empty fairgrounds. A discarded candy wrapper scampered across the dirt.

Emily took Pete's arm and leaned her weight against him slightly. Together they strolled past the carnival.

"How can I thank you enough, Pete, for all you've done?"

"Buy me a beer," he said.

They headed for the beer tent.

Epilogue

By the time you receive this letter,
you will already suspect
my ending and your beginning.
Stories are rarely what they seem.
While falcons reel
out of sight among clouds,
the downy dove fluffs her nest
by the silvery light from the moon.
Would that we were orphans
cast adrift from
our fathers' eternal blood thirst
to suckle at the breast
of Mother Earth!
Go forth, my child,
borne on wings of love.

The End

Printed in the United States
By Bookmasters